A FLOWER

AMONG

THE GOLD

A FLOWER

AMONG

THE GOLD

REALMS OF ERDARIS Series:

Volume One

Michael Patrick

Editing by Michelle Perez Montaner

Beta Reading & Content Editing Thanks to Shiloh VDL

Special Publication Thanks to Rich Wickliffe, Michael Palma Esq., Jose Lugo, Rory Giovino & Audiobook Voice Credit to Jackie Lastra

ISBN 978-1-7345608-0-0 (eBook)

ISBN 978-1-7345608-1-7 (Paperback)

ISBN 978-1-7345608-2-4 (Audiobook)

DEDICATION & ACKNOWLEDGMENT

To the strong, caring women in my life that have made me the person that I am today and continuously remind me to be better with each passing day.

To my mother, my mom... thank you for always being there for me and continuing to be with me through all of life's obstacles. I wouldn't be here if it wasn't for you (literally). From grade school to college, and then after, you've always guided me through it all with your compassion, encouragement, and understanding. I owe you the world.

To my wife, my honey... you're without a doubt, the most inspiring person I've ever met and you truly are my better half. You're kind yet strong, gentle but firm, and even though I'm a lot heavier than you, you still manage to be my shoulder to lean on every day. You're always there for me and my only hope is to always be there for you.

To my brave grandmothers... I'll try, but words can't describe how grateful I am that you both took the greatest risk one could ever ask for. You sacrificed everything you had for our sake by fleeing from oppression to grant us a better life in this democratic country we now call home. You were immigrants, minorities in an unknown state, but you still managed to provide, care, and nurture us with love into who we are today. Abella, I miss you every day; time hasn't gotten easier since you left us and I wish you were still here with me just like you were each moment of my childhood and thereafter. Mama, each day you're with me is a blessing, one I'm eternally thankful for and I promise to stay by your side through your golden years.

To my sister... the definition of tough and independent. I may be the big brother, but you're the strong one I go to for everything; from a laugh, to a simple conversation, and even a hug. I miss that you moved away, but I'm so happy that you still stay close like you never left.

To each and every one of you, the inspiring women in my life, thank you and from the bottom of my heart, I love you.

Lastly, a very special thanks to my family & friends for their continued support; and you, the reader, for picking up a copy. I hope you enjoy this work and the more to come from the REALMS OF ERDARIS series.

TABLE OF CONTENTS

Be mindful of the water around this delicate flower

CHAPTER ONE:

"AWAKEN"

G olden and bright was the sunlight that peeked through the humble home's eastward window, while loud and fervent were the tiny steps that pattered through its hallway. Coming at full force, the resounding pace did not relent until the nearest door endured a harsh push.

"Momma! Poppa!" called an excited little child aloud as she barged into her parent's silent room.

Tossing and turning while pretending to ignore his frantic daughter in hopes of continuing his sleep, the father only squirmed as he grunted, "Ugh."

Although he lazily disregarded his child with a tiresome attitude, the mother did not. Instead, the young and vibrant woman forcefully lifted herself up from the cotton-lined bed. As she brushed her blinking blue eyes and sat up, she remarked, "Cora, honey," pausing to yawn and swipe the

1

golden-brown hair away from her brow, the kind mother then went on, "It's still early."

"Sorry, Momma," responded the child as she stepped towards the right side of the bed where her mother sat. Despite slowing her feet to a near crawl, she begged in a slightly loud voice as she was clearly thrilled, "But the first day of fall. Today, it-it's today."

"I understand," uttered the patient mother, "but your father and I were sleeping." Picking Cora up and sitting her atop the soft sheets of cotton, the comforting mother continued alluding to the recent sunrise as she caressed her child's long and light, golden hair, "And your new schooling doesn't begin for almost two hours."

Staring into Cora's eyes that hinted of her own color, the mother became somewhat lost in thought. Soon, she joyfully smirked, then nodded as she saw the unrelenting excitement within the eight-year-old. She, too, began to give in – allowing eagerness to take hold.

Despite being delicate of touch and gentle in looks, Cora's mother had somewhat hardened hands and a firmness in her arms. Easily after sharing a wink, she was able to cradle her daughter around, then set her down between the hardy father and her slender figure. Leaning in, she kindly requested with a peaceful smile, "Now you stay here with Poppa and make sure he wakes while I prepare breakfast."

After pecking her smiling child on the forehead, the soft-spoken mother stood up and laid her feet upon the creaking wood floor. As she settled into a pair of old and worn leathery sandals, she pat down her night dress, then put her hands onto her daughter's smaller digits, offering, "I'll make us your favorite. Only the best for our little flower before her first day."

2

Springing up after the remark, Cora stood and jumped on the bed, forcing another grunt from her father, but a giggle from the loving mother.

Yet, despite the joy they shared, the dutiful mother put her index finger to her mouth – gently requesting some silence for the father with a light hush. Going over to him, the mother then reassured after warmly kissing him on the cheek, "Cehdric, love. Take some time before getting up, just enough so we can walk Cora before we're due in the north gardens."

As the caring woman raised the blanket over her exhausted husband's arms, Cehdric smiled, only offering, "Mhmm."

Excitedly, Cora watched as her mother made her exit – perching herself restlessly next to her father as he tried to gain the last few minutes of rest. Unable to restrain her enthusiasm, she blurted aloud near her father's ear, "Momma's making our favorite!"

"Hmm," responded Cehdric with an apathetic undertone. Despite his desire to continue sleeping, he grunted, then turned over to his daughter, kindly begging, "Momma's going to be a bit preparing it, won't you rest here just a little with Poppa until it's ready?"

"Alright," returned Cora with a nod as she slid down over the covers. While twiddling her toes and fiddling with her fingers, she joyfully continued, "But Momma said."

"And I promise I'll be up," affirmed Cehdric who now shared a tired, but happy grin with his child. "Who'd want to miss the food?"

Leaning over to her, the waking father went in to tickle Cora's stomach while adding, "Not our little tulip's belly, that's for certain."

Although he had a mild spurt of animation, Cehdric dropped back down to rest his head atop the fluffed pillows as

3

he finished, "But for now, a smidge of rest until we're off to school, hmm?"

Cheerfully, Cora agreed – laying her head down just the same as her father, but not before widely grinning at him and expressing her joy. Quietly, she watched as he drifted back into slumber – witnessing him lightly snoring and twitching as sleep took hold. Too, she would begin to feel her liveliness fade as the room was now silent.

With her father speechless in his respite, Cora switched her gaze – tossing upright to then stare onto the ceiling. Attempting to occupy herself and resist falling into hibernation as her father had, she started to count. First, she began with the nails that held the beams upright, then went onto the cracks that were lined with a light dew from the morning's mist seeping through it.

In spite of her attempts, Cora's eyelids began to grow heavy while sluggishly spouting, "Eleven... twelve." Her blinks became slower, her breath deeper. Soon, she found herself drifting – being called deep into her dreams, but then suddenly being jolted out of it.

"Hey there, sleepy," uttered the father softly while gently caressing the top of her head. "It's time."

Lifting herself up, Cora first saw her father who was wide awake and dressed in his horticulturist attire. As the sun peeked from behind, she glinted her eyes, then offered, "But. But, I just closed my eyes."

"I know, tulip," remarked Cehdric while picking up his daughter and setting her tiny feet on the ground. As she reached an inch over his belly button, he now looked down while continuing, "We'd better hurry, breakfast's going to get cold. And don't you worry," uttered Cehdric as he fastened his collar with a smirk. "Momma's going to be proud you made sure I was up in time."

Initiating a step, the kind father lastly nudged, "Now let's get a move on, shall we."

Eagerly, Cora nodded in return – quickly stepping in front, then leading as they made a right down the simplistic, wood-lined hallway that carried a sweet aroma. Rapidly passing the lone desk in the passage, she cleared it and rushed to the door's arch where the smell grew stronger, zipping left and lastly into the kitchen where her mother stood.

"Now Cora, no running," lightly reminded the mother. As she went over to stop her daughter in her tracks, she went on, "Wouldn't want you bumping into our table and hurting yourself or spilling it all, right?"

Moving aside while Cora was halted and nodding in agreement, the kind mother stepped out to reveal the elaborate display on the dining table. The savory scent that called to her in the hall was now burning into her eyes and overwhelming her senses. Lunging forward, she hastily sat atop the nearest chair of carved oak, then peered with a grand appetite upon the assortment of cinnamon sweet toast, red and blue wildberries, and the two jars that stood at their ends.

Without hesitation, the famished Cora reached for two red berries, tossing them towards her mouth. Although she missed one that flew by her, the other was soon chomped, forcing the dark crimson juice to gush out partially onto her lips. Smiling at the feat, her mother reached for a cloth rag and plate, then for the larger of the two jars – pouring a cupful of fresh, white milk, then another.

As Cora leaned in further, she grasped three slices of sweet toast, then began to force one towards her teeth as the polite mother once more softly mentioned, "Now, now. Do you recall your manners at the table?"

"Yes, Momma," remarked the excited, but apologetic child after shaking her head in atonement while allowing her mother to set the plate and napkin next to the iron fork and knife. "I'm sorry."

"There's no need to be, we're at home," comforted the loving mother who brought the other jar closer with one hand as she stroked her daughter's hair with the other. "Just remember to be polite in school and mindful of your manners when you're around others."

With her mother's eyes hinting towards the freshly prepared food, Cora was given permission to continue. Licking her chops and happily agreeing, she then reached for the smaller jar and slathered her toast in a golden, honey syrup while her father joined in after lagging behind.

"Aeyra, dear," he greeted while picking up a cup of milk and sharing a kiss, "I'll be out front gathering all we need before we go. Any seeds?" he asked.

"Just the tools," confirmed the mother who joyfully smirked as she watched Cora dig into her food. While a long strand of the honey syrup dripped down onto her child's fingers, she giggled, then turned once more to her husband as she mentioned, "Just don't forget the smaller spade."

Confirming the request, Cehdric then went off towards the back of the house, but not before he was stopped as Aeyra added, "And the shears! All of them this time."

"Mhmm," waved the father – continuing his pace outward after acknowledging his wife.

Now turning back towards her daughter, the diligent mother uttered, "I'll be off collecting your things for school. Just be sure to wash up after you finish your toast."

"And Misses Moo's milk," blurted out Cora as she grinned widely with a layer of white that lined her mouth.

Although her mother smiled, she turned to a slight sadness as she reminisced with the touch of her daughter's hair,

"Misses Moo is still at home, tulip. But this is from one of her friends who want to make sure you grow nice and tall."

"Mister Moo?" begged Cora.

Holding back a chuckle, Aeyra only offered her smile as she took a moment to comment, "We'll have all the time from the door to the great big magister building to talk about her friends. Just be ready in a few for Momma, will you?"

With Cora's acknowledgment, the mother then parted from the kitchen – leaving her alone to tend to the unfinished berries and sweet-baked bread. Somewhat clumsily, she cut up another few pieces and stuffed them in her mouth one by one, until they were all swallowed almost whole by the small child who clearly had quite the appetite.

"Ah," she gasped – taking in a large breath before she finished. "All done, Momma!"

Standing onto her two feet, Cora perked up, then grabbed her plate, but not before uttering, "Oh."

Staring at the mostly empty cup of milk, she felt her thirst. Being called by the alluring ceramic jar, she reached for it with both hands. Although her mother was able to easily pour with one hand, Cora struggled – using both to manage the handle as she at first got more on the table than in the container.

Eventually, the milk filled to the brim and Cora began to lay the handle back but noticed the jar suddenly got heavier – forcing her to lose her balance while a splash of its contents poured out. As she struggled, the ceramic piece only grew more weighted, causing her to spill more of the liquid that was now changing from a thick white to thin and clear. Frightened by the jug, Cora instinctively dropped it – landing it perfectly on the wooden floor with an eerie thud that failed to crack its base.

Although it stood upright, the ceramic jar kept overflowing with water now from all sides, soon covering the floor in a puddle that kept rising from Cora's toes, to the top of her foot, then onto her ankle.

Frantically, she screamed for her mother and father, but no answer was returned.

Panicked, she leaned down – shoving her hands down to surround the jar's lip, but the water pushed back with increased vigor.

"Momma! Poppa!" she cried – erupting in tears as the flow started to force her hands upward and away from the ceaselessly spouting container.

"Momma!" she kept on as the jar rattled and shook – causing her body to sway.

Harsh was the current, fierce its pull, and loud its sound, only slightly slowing as a deep voice emanated through the rush, "Cora! Get up, tulip!"

From within the jar, two hairy arms came out – grasping her at the shoulders and pulling her inward, to the deep and dark, overflowing center of the jar.

Violently, Cora was jerked upright as the kitchen, even the jar faded, but only the arms remained – ones that now became surrounded by her father's figure first, then her parents' east-facing bedroom and its walls.

Concerned, the recently awakened Cehdric looked upon his child after calling for Aeyra from the kitchen and said, "You're safe, we're here."

Unable to restrain her tears, Cora only breathed heavily while anxiously rattling atop the bed sheets as Cehdric leaned in closer to cradle her.

"We're here," comforted the father while embracing and assuring his daughter. "Nothing's going to hurt you, we're here."

Rushing in, Aeyra dismissed her usual, calm demeanor and sprinted towards the opposite side of the bed to hug her petrified child who was in a state of speechless shock. Without regard for all else, she bumped the nightstand and leaned in closer, sitting next to Cora and tightly clinging to her.

After uttering a few calm, easing words to her child, Aeyra then turned upward to stare at the ceiling – witnessing some of the falling dew that pelted the bed where her daughter laid.

Shifting Cora closer into her arms, Aeyra then questioned towards her husband, "Another one? I was only gone for a moment." As he affirmed, she went on in a concerned whisper, "They're getting worse, she needs to be seen."

Nodding his head, Cehdric attested in a low voice, "There's no better place than here. They promised if we came, they'd help."

Now looking upon his daughter whose nerves were soothing throughout the passing seconds, he kissed her forehead and concluded, "There's nothing we won't do for our little tulip."

CHAPTER TWO:

"FROM ONE DOOR TO THE OTHER"

C rack went the oval-shaped door as a pair of calloused hands pulled the planks inward. With a light movement, the hinges sang as a tiny, carved hummingbird first went through, then the small hand that held it, and lastly, the rest of the girl's body. Quietly and mournfully, the child stepped onto the paved stone as she looked down – only staring at her trinket while her other arm held in the doorway.

Following the hushed footsteps of her distressed daughter, Aeyra emerged. Although she carried with her a hint of sadness, she set aside the gloom and kept at Cora's side while holding her with one hand and in the other, having a bundled napkin that was lightly stained from a red and blue juice. During her stride, the cloth piece dangled, releasing a sweet smell of cinnamon and freshly baked bread that overpowered the scented wildberries they were paired with.

"Cora, honey," insisted Aeyra with a kindness amid her concern. "You should eat, even if it's only a bit."

Turning upward to face her mother, the rosy-cheeked, listless Cora only maintained a pouted expression. Her frown and the dried tears along her cheeks held as she responded in a low, pensive tone, "I'm not hungry."

"Nonsense," grinned Cehdric as he followed them out with a tender smile and a more positive expression. "Our little tulip's always hungry for her favorite." Bending down slightly and putting both hands on his knees as the door shut behind him, he went on, "Just a bite? At least for Momma and Poppa," now looking at the wooden figure in her palm, he finished, "And Chirpy."

Although she kept her head down and lingered on with a withdrawn sentiment as all initiated their walk, Cora agreed. Removing her hand from her mother's grasp, she somewhat perked up, then extended her arm outward. With a smile, Aeyra nodded and motioned to a loaf of sweet bread, but went for a few berries instead after Cora shook her head towards the larger treat.

As she placed a small handful of the plump fruits in her daughter's palm, Aeyra cheerfully remarked, "A few for you, and the rest for our friend."

"Momma," retorted Cora as she chomped, "you know Chirpy can't eat."

"I know, dear, yet look at where we are," reminded Aeyra gently as she retied the napkin's knot. Gesturing towards the grand and illustrious structures that surrounded them, she went on, "This place is full of magic, anything's possible."

"Not entirely sure that's how it works," commented Cehdric as he kept slightly behind in pace while shouldering his dirt-lined supply sack.

While Aeyra turned back to scold her husband's uncalled for humor, Cora uttered with her head hanging low, "They'll be able to fix me then."

Turning around instantly, the loving mother halted in her steps – forcing Cora to turn towards her.

"There's nothing wrong that needs fixing," assured Aeyra as she embraced her whimpering child. While a pair of tears now ran down her own cheek, she continued while warmly staring into Cora's blue eyes, "You're perfect just how you are."

Weeping softly, Cora only muttered, "But we left home because of me."

Still caressing her child, Aeyra noticed Cora's earlier excitement that was being built up for school was fading as a familiar mild fear and hesitation took hold, causing her to rebut as the nurturing matriarch that she was, "Cora, honey… you're our world, just there's some matters Poppa and I can't teach. That nice magister who came to our home told us just how gifted you are and she invited us – for you to attend the best school in all of the cities. Nothing's broken, there's only the magic within you that needs some training and understanding is all."

As Cora lunged her small arms around her mother to return with an invigorated hug and a smile, Cehdric ran off but remained within both their sights while striding towards a nearby, well-maintained brush and tree. Reaching into the flowers, he plucked out a blossoming white tulip, then rushed back to his daughter and joined in on the final moments of the embrace.

Now pulling back from the tender hold, Cehdric grabbed Cora's left hand, placing the blooming bulb into her palm as he complimented, "This tulip isn't as lovely or special as our very own little flower, but it'll get Chirpy's beak acquainted for when you're a great, big magister and can make it all possible."

Although Cora smiled and placed the two together – her figurine and the flower – Aeyra let out a mildly crossed expression. While Cehdric attempted to withdraw his prior statement on magic that upset her, Aeyra interrupted, sharing her concern in a low voice for their daughter to barely hear, "You'll be fined if they saw you, why'd you do that?"

Listening to his wife, Cehdric only pointed out the lifted spirits of Cora and the unaware crowds that flocked intently to the nearby market, but Aeyra insisted in a somewhat more eased tone, "Just be careful, we don't have even a single copper for any penalties. This isn't home where we can…"

"Do as we did before," interjected Cehdric in a pensive voice. "I know. Yet," continuing while both joyfully turned to Cora, Cehdric went on, "if it means replanting or tending to more patches, I'll do it… we'll do it, for her."

Sharing a wide smile, Aeyra gleefully agreed and added in a louder tone for her daughter to acknowledge the late time, "And that means walking her to school early for as long as we're able."

Jesting, Cehdric commented, "Even if she's older and grows embarrassed of us, we'll still be there."

Having listened to her parents, Cora set aside the momentary play between her hummingbird and the tulip to look up, then reassure with a cheerful grin and squinted eyes, "I'll never get tired of walking with Momma and Poppa."

Patting her gently, Cehdric chuckled as Aeyra smirked. While they all sought to enjoy one another's company for as much as possible within the mostly residential section of the capital, the dutiful mother reminded once more of avoiding tardiness – causing the trio to resume their pace atop the clean and sculpted, stony streets of the northeast section.

13

On they went, strolling ahead of the smaller gardens and the adjoined homes, then diving into the bustling market. Although they were kindly saluted and greeted by peddlers of fine wares, the polite family only offered their courteous refusal. Respectful as all were, none gave pursuit or further solicitation. Rather, the gathered citizens humbly allowed the three through without delay.

In little time, the two parents led Cora past the commotion and toward the opened, adorned gate that divided their section from the central portion. As they crossed, a noticeable change was felt – one where the uproar from content commoners was replaced by the clanking of metal boots as files of infantry marched near the mostly silent nobles who passed them.

"Look, Momma!" pointed Cora as she gazed in awe at the coordination of the armored soldiers that strode by them in perfect harmony.

Despite being equally as intrigued and drawn to the high level of organization, Aeyra kept her focus – ushering her daughter, even her astonished husband, away from the military formation. Pressing them to mind the hour, she guided the two bewildered members of her family past the immense barracks and armory, then onto the next illustrious building that caused an even longer pause.

"Ooh," mumbled Cora as she stared up in wonder.

"Now that's a sight," joined the father who also looked up alongside his daughter.

The two seemed stupefied, caught in a long gaze over the regal palace of the High King and Queen – one that even caused Aeyra to momentarily disregard her hurry and join in.

"Ah," Cora followed with clear excitement as she moved her head side-to-side to see the wide-spanning building, then shifted upward to gawk at the central spire that seemed so tall to her that it could pierce the sky.

Patting his child's shoulder gently, Cehdric added, "Looks much bigger here than from our window, eh?"

Although the three shared a profound wonder for the glorious structure, the mindful mother recalled, "Cora, we mustn't be late, honey."

Affirming his wife's statement, Cehdric nodded, but still kept his eyes fixed on the majestic architecture and its flawless design. With a poke from his loving spouse, he awakened – begging Cora come along while promising that as they settle within their new home, they will relish in its wonders when they have ample time.

In spite of her desire to keep the two on pace, Aeyra slowed her quickening steps and agreed – reinforcing the forthcoming sightseeing and even adding a sweet and savory market treat or two for their daughter's delight.

As smiles and joyful sentiments were received to the idea, the mother furthered cheerfully, "We're almost there, just a bit more."

Heralding them to the north and west, Aeyra strode with her husband and daughter in tow – moving them beyond the lengthy marvel of the capital and towards another beautiful structure of equal size that sparked further stares and slightly slowed steps. Yet, the mother pressed, guaranteeing that there would be plenty of time to revel in its splendor as it was the grandiose library linked to Cora's school.

Listening to her mother, Cora only bounced her head up and down in agreement, but it did not take away from her focus as she gazed upon the circular building's majestic design and its shimmering dome of glass. "So shiny," she complimented.

"That it is," added Cehdric in a childish glee while looking up and briefly stopping. "Simply amazing."

15

Not halting her steps while holding Cora's hand, Aeyra only reminded, "Cehdric, the time."

"Yes, yes," responded the father in a much more mature tone than his prior statement. "You're right, apologies," he atoned.

Pushing past its round shape, Aeyra led with a greater rush around the side of the westernmost building within the inner section of the capital. As she saw other parents making their exit from its end, she only rushed further while asking her husband and daughter do the same to avoid tardiness.

Under the mother's haste, the three reached the northern building that was attached to the spherical library in just a pair of minutes. Quickly, they descended upon its westward facing entrance as the last pair of a mother and father departed.

Sensing his wife's urgency, Cehdric rushed forward – pressing to the first elven guard nearest the adorned inward passage. "Tell me class hasn't begun yet," he begged with a squint as the tall sentry's plate armor painted in gold and silver reflected the morning sun back at him.

At first, Cehdric politely waited for a response from the High Elf, but no words were offered. Instead, the silent guard continued to stare outward through his open-faced helmet while firmly holding his long, ironsteel pike.

Joining her husband to move him along from the motionless ward, Aeyra stepped near to pull him away, but was halted in her words as an echo rang from the passage.

"The student is not as early as the rest, nor is she tardy," interjected a warm female voice who emerged from the adorned archway.

Stepping out into the light, the instructor's elegantly sleeved dress of amber and maroon first caught the human family's eye, but soon they shifted to her long ears that peeked out from her thinning cherry brown and white-streaked hair. With her last step, another switch in gaze was forced as she lowered her scarred left hand that blotted out the sunlight – revealing to the two parents the face of the older elf who once visited them.

Continuing on from her words, the elder magister went on in her formal tone, "The Everstone family, we are glad that you made the trip to join us." Looking to the father and mother, she greeted, "It is a pleasure to once more see you."

Now bending her neck down slightly, she softly added while staring at the daughter, "And we are especially delighted to have you here, Cora Everstone. Welcome to The Magister's School of the Gilded Highborn… or 'The School', as we simply call it."

While Cora only silently smiled, Cehdric asked, "You do remember the nice Arch Magister who spoke to us of your enrollment, don't you?"

"Misses Ashy-mane?" recalled Cora with a slight stumble after looking to her mother first.

Lightly chuckling, the elven magister corrected, "Quite close, though I am simply a Miss and it is pronounced Ashmane. Although that is my proper name, I do request I be referred to as Head Instructor now that you are one of our wonderful students." As Cora continued her cheerful grin, she furthered, "This is an exciting moment now that you are here with us, the first year of your magister's curriculum awaits. Are you ready?"

Still maintaining her smile, Cora nodded rapidly once, twice, then a third time, but looked to her two parents for their approval. As both gave their consent, Aeyra bent down to caress her child while Cehdric leaned in with a forward pace – forcing the once still guard's motion.

"My apologies," halted the Arch Magister. Hinting to the halfway mark between the second and third hour after sunrise, she continued, "Class is to begin shortly and we ask that only students and Instructors be present while we are in session."

Holding her mother tightly, Cora only let go when her mother pulled back and said, "We'll be right here when you're dismissed and you can tell us all about how well your day went over some market treats on our way home, hmm?"

"Mhmm," agreed Cora as she leaned back in to hug her mother once more.

As the two finished their embrace, Cehdric joined in, offering, "And we'll be sure to be here early enough next time so we can see your classroom and meet your new friends."

Despite the tender moment that she did not wish to interrupt, the Arch Magister made a lightly gestured cough to remind of the time. With a nod from her family, Cora went over to the Instructor's side, but not before grabbing a small pack and the bundled sweet bread from her parents.

"Momma," asked Cora, "is it alright if I eat just one and share the rest?"

Smiling proudly in return, Aeyra replied, "Of course, tulip."

"While we provide all a student should require, including an assortment of delicacies from our kitchens," added Arch Magister Ashmane, "I am certain your classmates will enjoy the treat." Placing her hand around Cora's shoulder and turning towards the illustrious passage inward, she concluded, "Now, shall we?"

CHAPTER THREE:

"THE FIRST DAY"

U nder the wing of The School's Head Instructor, Cora was ushered down the elegant hallway and away from her waving parents who smiled with a light, hopeful sob. Although she stared back, the slightly darker, yet well-lit passage darkened her mother and father's silhouette, soon forcing her to turn and face the direction she traveled toward.

Now more attentive to her surroundings, Cora focused on the decorated walls she quickly paced through. Covered end to end, she stared at the adornments she was not accustomed to seeing – from fine art and literature, to statue busts, and stained oak. The shimmer and elegance of each object drew her so much that she even started to gasp in wonder and slow herself to absorb the memory of each design.

Yet, Cora was sped up as the gentle, but firm voice of the Arch Magister reminded, "The mid hour approaches." Sensing the curious spirit in the child, she kindly continued,

"However, I assure that there shall be plenty of time to make yourself familiar with each wondrous intricacy as you study alongside us. Now," she carried on, "your classroom is just a tad further down and on the left."

"Yes, Miss Head Instructor," confirmed Cora with a tender tone after nodding twice.

As her instinct was to correct the student when it came to her title, the Head Instructor opened her mouth with a mumble, but halted her words. Returning the smile instead, she carried on in a soft-spoken tone, "Here we are."

Pointing upward, Head Instructor Ashmane shifted Cora's focus towards the large door to her classroom. Pushing it inward, the courteous elf held the richly carved frame – allowing the young pupil to enter before her.

Letting out another light gasp, Cora was startled as she looked upon the lively room full of children that were engaged in conversation and play. Quickly, her attention then shifted to the plainly dressed Instructor that approached from the head of the class.

"Welcome, welcome," said the kind man as he placed both hands in an inverted manner atop his hips and the cracked leather belt that held his trousers together. With his brown eyes fixed onto the small child, he continued, "Always happy to see a new student joining us."

While Cora smiled, the gentle Instructor ushered her further inward, then went on to his elven superintendent, "You have my thanks, Astrael. And a good morning to you."

"To you as well, Loswick," returned the Arch Magister. "This is Cora Everstone, the last arrival for the day."

One final time, the Head Instructor looked to the young child, then bid her farewell, "I leave you in good hands."

As the Arch Magister hustled off into the hallway, the human teacher introduced, "Delighted to meet you, Miss

Everstone, my name is Instructor Pepperton. I am here to guide you on your exciting first year with us."

While she looked up to the polite and proper man, Cora bashfully nodded as the classroom door now completely shut at her side – forcing a slight hesitation since the last familiar face faded away just as her parents recently had.

Sensing a familiar behavior from his new student, Instructor Pepperton commented with his light-hearted voice, "Almost thirty years ago, I stood right there in my little shoes. I was a bit anxious to be away from my family, but that quickly faded when I met my new friends and saw how nice everyone was. So what do you say, shall we get acquainted with your fellow classmates?"

Bobbing her head up and down, Cora then went forward under the teacher's direction as he pointed out an open seat in the rear row. With a growing smile that mostly calmed her nerves, she made her way down the middle aisle of slightly older children that greeted her as an equal.

"Hello," said the first.

"Nice to me-meet you," stuttered the next.

"Is that cinnamon?" asked a chubby third.

"Smells like it! We can all share! My own mother packed me a bundle of..." exclaimed the eccentric last, but was unable to finish as she was politely hushed by the teacher.

"Now, now," announced the Instructor with a mild boom in his voice, "if we can all quiet down for a moment and take our seats, we will begin our journey into the breathtaking world of magic."

Although his voice was kind, Instructor Pepperton's tone was commanding enough to garner the attention of each and every child. With all calmly in their seats, he pondered aloud on his last word, "Ah, magic..." Grasping the wooden wand that sat on his belt, the composed teacher reached into his chalk-lined pocket as he continued, "The very essence and reason why we are all here."

Throwing his hand outward and away from his trousers, the Instructor released a flicker of light after a word from an oddly-spoken language. The children watched in glee and with a delightful cheer as the small spark twisted into the shape of a box with a glowing ribbon. Although it faded as fast as it flared, it still gathered the amusement of all for a short time, until the Instructor continued his speech.

"It is a gift," he said. "Just as you all are. A gift we are here to nurture, to grow, and to learn about together. Although I am here to instruct you during your first year, you are all here to teach me as well. We will learn from each other and about one another as we become acquainted with this fascinating world.

"And speaking of becoming acquainted," continued Instructor Pepperton while turning to the large, rectangular parchment that ran along the wall behind him. Looking towards his name that was eloquently written in a dark chalk atop the beige paper, then back to the students, he carried on, "You all now know who I am, so it is time for us to learn a tad about each other."

Setting his stare upon Cora, the Instructor courteously gestured the youngest of his pupils to rise while saying, "This classroom has a little tradition where the last to enter, closes the door behind them so that we may initiate or resume our lessons for the day. Although you were all here timely, Miss Everstone, you were the last to step through. For this activity, I will ask you to join me at the front of the class so that rather than close the door, we can open one – an entrance to letting your fellow classmates know a little about you."

As she took a step, Cora first lowered her head in a bashful manner, but rapidly raised it as Instructor Pepperton

22

continued, "I will start with a tidbit about me, then you can help me by introducing yourself and picking the next student to come up. A little game for us all – what do you say?"

Cheerfully, Cora nodded. Although her steps were short due to being petite at an inch short of four feet, she sped up her pace fast enough to quickly join the side of the much taller Instructor.

After a light cheer for the first student at the front of the classroom, Instructor Pepperton began, "As I look at all of you today, it takes me back to my first day... a first day where I had the silliest hair in the room." As the youthful pupils began to giggle, he continued, "My hair was tied in knots and bands, but the day was humid and my curls just kept coming out. All the fuzzy, pokey hairs, they just kept popping out of the ties as the day went on. Mister Frizzyton, that is what they called me in my first year." While the children laughed, the gleeful Instructor continued to share, "You see, I grew up in our northwest border at the Shimmering Fort. My mother thought it fashionable to dress me with a Vjordic look – a style she later abandoned in favor of what many of you are wearing today. One I am happy for, as my hair just never cooperated with any warmer temperature."

Around the room, the chuckles soon shifted to stares of curiosity as the children looked to one another – inspecting the simplistic style of clothing and hairstyles they had, from free-flowing cuts and ponytails to tattered dresses and stitched shirts. Despite their attentiveness to one another's appearance, their focus was once more altered as Mister Pepperton said, "Now that you all know a little more about me, it is time to learn about Miss Everstone." Looking to the student at his side, he kindly finished, "You have the classroom, my lady."

"Umm," thought the child as she pat down her dress, then crossed her hands behind her leggings, "I'm Cora, I'm eight-years-old and I'm from…"

Although she tried to finish her sentence, Cora was interrupted by a pair of students.

"From Arulan where they speak like that?"

"Two years early, so lucky," they blurted.

Stepping forward, Instructor Pepperton urged calm as he requested, "Class, there will be plenty of time to get to know one another throughout the school year. Let us hold the questions and comments for now and allow Cora to speak, yes?"

As the room full of children acknowledged, Instructor Pepperton gave his signal to carry on, prompting Cora to resume in her lower tone, "I'm from Riverbend, in…. umm, the south. Really close to Ar-Arala…"

"Arulan," chimed in Pepperton.

"We have a home there where Momma and Poppa grow flowers, and plants, and trees," continued Cora in a shy manner. "Poppa's the gardener and Momma's a ba-banotomy master."

"Botany," corrected the Instructor with a smile, one that gave Cora a sense of ease after she momentarily got stuck on another word.

"Momma and Poppa," she went on as the nervousness of being at the center of attention began to diminish, "came up here. We moved for school. We have a cow, Misses Moo, but she couldn't come with us. She stayed at home to keep it ready for when Clucky's chicken family returns. Momma said they went off to help make sure we, and all our friends, have dinner every night and will come back when I'm bigger." Looking back to her desk, she pointed at the wooden figurine as she lastly said, "And that's Chirpy."

Smiling at her innocence, Instructor Pepperton said, "And we are glad your family and Chirpy have come to join us within the Golden Citadel. Thank you, Miss Everstone." After invoking a round of applause and a brief congratulations, he furthered, "Now if you please, select another one of our wonderful students to join us in our introduction game."

Seeing the kind and generous nature of the teacher, many children raised their hands – requesting Cora pick them to be the next at the front of the class.

"Me!"

"No, me!"

"Me, me, me!" they shouted.

After a hum and a twist of her left foot, Cora settled her eyes. Pointing to the rear of the room, she picked the dark-haired, lively girl who sat in front of her.

"Thank you!" exclaimed the child through her grin that had a gap where her two front teeth should be. Dashing up the middle aisle, she ran to the head of the room and right up to Cora. Easily, the taller, older, and slightly wider girl was able to wrap her arms around and embrace the thinly-framed student from Riverbend. "I am Emmie," she introduced after expressing her appreciation and letting go of her newfound friend. Alluding to Cora's slender figure that barely reached fifty pounds, Emmie pressed on, "My mother gave me a whole bag of pumpkin toffee, we should share." Turning to the classroom, Emmie finished, "All of us."

Stunned with happiness, Cora only nodded while she stood in silence. In response to the classroom's erupting cheer, she then offered the sweet, cinnamon delights her Momma had packed along with the red and blue wildberries.

Prompted by the kind gestures, Instructor Pepperton said, "Sharing is a part of life… a part that strengthens our joy, our spirits, and our friends. Although 'The School' provides all you shall need for class – from food and refreshments, to the books, parchment, and the very ink used to write on them – it is important to share that which makes us unique. Our tastes, our stories, and our friendship, all of that is encouraged here."

Switching his attention to the youngest in his room, Instructor Pepperton concluded, "Now if you would be so kind, Miss Everstone, please return to your seat so that Miss Tenderlyn may share a little about herself with the class."

Happily, Cora agreed – trotting with joy back to her desk where she would attentively listen to her new friend, then the next student, and the following until all of the children had their turn at introducing themselves in front of the classroom. Patiently, she listened to all, even taking some scribbled notes on the old parchment and worn feather that her Poppa had given her.

When all was done after a few additional morning exercises, the Instructor gathered all of the students' attention. After asking them to rise, he led them out the door and into the winding corridor that was full of other classrooms, then towards an aromatic trail that hinted of sweet and savory delights. Onward to a large set of double doors they went, ones that seemed to part on their own when they arrived.

To Cora's amazement, a magnificent banquet hall was revealed with dozens of finely engraved tables and scores of intricately carved chairs that were being filled by older magister trainees and their Instructors as they rushed towards them. Despite most focusing on the impending meal, Cora could not help but stand in awe as she noticed her wondrous surroundings. First, she set her eyes on the hanging dragon banners of the Golden Realm that draped the walls and the stained glass windows that stood by them. Then, she tilted her head upwards to fix her gaze on the rich oak beams along the ceiling and the candle-filled chandeliers they held.

Focused and intrigued, Cora kept staring at it all but was diverted to a nearby table as the Instructor called her attention. In little time, she found an empty chair, then faded back to looking at the impressive designs around her – the lavish silverware, the adorned platters that awaited their delicacies, and even the tiles of etched stone that covered the floor.

Soon, Cora's concentration was changed once more as the lovely scent of freshly baked loaves arrived. Accompanied by freshly churned butter and fruit jams, the crisp muffins and rolls called to all at the table. Yet, it was a mere sample as the true feast quickly followed. An assortment of roasted vegetables, herb-stuffed poultry, golden apples, succulent white grapes, and honey-flavored refreshments were laid down in a grand presentation that awed the first year students and the older ones alike.

After everyone in the grand hall had their fill, the students began to be dismissed in an orderly fashion – with Instructor Pepperton's to be at the forefront as they were the junior class. In little time, they rejoined at their classroom to continue onto the next portion of their schedule – receiving their books and supplies.

With the minutes and hours passing rather quickly for those on their inaugural day, Instructor Pepperton felt it was due to remind all of the time. Following the last set of feathered quills that were handed out, he announced, "As much as I have enjoyed our introductory lessons, I am afraid we are nearing a quarter before the third hour after midday, which means we must be readying ourselves for dismissal." Grabbing a pair of books, he provided an example as he continued, "Underneath your seats, you may store your books

27

and supplies atop the basket. Please ensure your desks are neat and cleared. For those of you that opted to stay within the dormitories, kindly remain at your seats to be ushered as a group since you will need to be formally acquainted with the facilities. Those with families living within the city, you may individually await your relatives or travel home as you desire. I shall remain until the last student departs and to prepare for the following day's lesson plan."

Heeding the instructions of their teacher, the attentive children went about the duties asked of them. As the room was tidied and a quarter-to-the-hour reached, Instructor Pepperton opened the classroom door – initiating the exit process for his students. To his surprise, two parents were already standing idly by with clear permission from the Arch Magister as they were already inside while most others were just being allowed in.

"It's nice to meet you, we're Cora's parents. May we wait here until she's ready?" asked the mother in a kind tone.

"So this is her classroom. We didn't get to…" said the father. After the mother interrupted him with a nudge, he corrected, "I mean, it's nice to meet you."

"The pleasure is mine," answered the tall Instructor with his more proper accent as he looked upon the two parents who were a decade younger than he. Pointing out their child in the middle aisle, he went on, "She has been a delight today." Bowing his head, he finished, "I thank you for raising such a sweet, kind, and thoughtful child – you should be proud of her. I look forward to instructing her this school year."

As the mother and father expressed their gratitude and exchanged their formal names with the teacher, Cora noticed them. Now being signaled by her Instructor, she rushed up in excitement to embrace both her parents simultaneously – a feat she could only accomplish with one arm to each as her small figure did not allow her to expand her grasp any further. Still, she tried, attempting to bring her parents closer in her animated state.

"Momma! Poppa!" Cora exclaimed as they all huddled. "There's so much to tell you, I love school, I can't wait for tomorrow and every day after that. There was a great big meal and I have new friends, and we shared snacks." Pulling herself back and extending her finger towards the other children who waved at her, she continued, "There's Emmie, then Joulen's the one in front of her, and Grayce just ahead of him. She's really nice and…"

On and on Cora continued, spouting off her fellow classmates as her Momma and Poppa listened intently. The two did their best to keep up with the slew of information, but their focus went from keeping track of the names to simply enjoying the happiness that emanated from their daughter. Both were so overjoyed with the positive news that Aeyra began to let out tears of relief, ones that caused Cora to apologize as she thought she had said something wrong during her speech.

"You needn't be sorry," remarked Aeyra. "We're just so glad that you had such a wonderful day." Lovingly, she went in to cradle her child in her arms. Then, she continued, "Now, let's head on home and get you cleaned up for supper. You can tell us all about the rest until it's time for bed."

"And we'll make sure we get you here early enough tomorrow so you can spend more time with your new friends in the morning," added Cehdric.

As Cora happily agreed, the parents took to her sides and held her hands. With elevated spirits and wide smiles, they initiated their walk away from the classroom and towards their humble cottage.

CHAPTER FOUR:

"IN THE BEGINNING"

After a short end of week rest that succeeded the first five school sessions, Instructor Pepperton awaited his returning students that joyfully trickled in on a bright and early morning. With the last student stepping inside, he said, "Good day, class." Looking towards the slender, pale-faced girl who closed the door that seemed somewhat heavy for her, he continued, "Thank you, Miss Delutton."

"Y-you are welcome," responded the girl in her kind, yet usual bashful stutter.

As the child went towards her second seat in the middle aisle, all the others gave their friendly greetings and went on with their excited school cheer, but their voices were drowned out by the commanding voice of their teacher. "Let us settle ourselves for a moment as I make a few announcements," he requested.

Listening to their elder, the students calmed themselves as Instructor Pepperton picked up a signed parchment from the Arch Magister. Carefully, he delivered the messages from his superior to the attentive pupils. Although some were important and others mundane, he broadcast it all the same and down to the last word. Having reached the bottom of the paper, he concluded, "Now that we have heard from the Head Instructor, it is time to move onto our scheduled lesson of the day."

Drawing a joyous applause from the children, Instructor Pepperton smiled, but once more asked for quiet as he said, "To learn about today, it is often important to delve into the past, where it all started. The start...," he paused. As the classful of children grew intrigued with wide eyes, he went on, "The beginning, when we first received the most precious gift we have – life."

Begging his students to rise, the kind teacher went on, "Today, I will ask you all to join me at the front of the class for a special presentation." As the first-year pupils paced forward, the Instructor then requested a pair of students to close the wooden window blinds while asking another set to assist him with a collection of blanketed mats.

After the comfortable padding was laid down, Instructor Pepperton asked the children to quietly sit and huddle alongside one another in a half circle while he went to stand at the front and center. With only a few shimmers of light peeking through the sealed, westward-facing windows, the children were barely able to see their teacher's face, but it was only temporary.

Having spouted a strange word, the Instructor released a glowing orb of light from his wand that was raised near his chin – illuminating his mouth and eyes while creating a dark silhouette around the outline of his head.

31

"For us to first understand life," he explained, "we must first learn of its origin."

Releasing the glowing orb high, Instructor Pepperton carried it up with his wand. While the class stared in fascination, he swooshed his instrument to force the ball into a winding spiral that carried high and splintered into five differently tinted tails.

As the shimmering swirl of red, white, blue, green, and yellow spun around, he began his story, "Countless millennia ago, there existed a Timeless Void where only these colors shone throughout the universe. Each represented an aspect of one of the five divine beings that lived among the heavens. These gods, or Dracozim as they became known to us, were alone – roaming an endlessly vast space where only they occupied the stars. Seeking an end to their solidarity, they agreed to use the great magical powers they were born of to create a world at the heart of their cosmos – one at a perfect distance from a nearby star."

Thrusting his wand in a downward motion amid the awed stares of his students, Instructor Pepperton combined the spinning streaks into a single flash of light in front of his chest. As a soft boom dazzled his audience, he revealed a solid mass that splintered off two smaller spheres – ones that stood a slight distance from its larger counterpart at the center.

"Thus, Erdaris and its moons came to be," he said.

Bringing his left hand underneath the middlemost orb as the right hand held above with his wand, the teacher enlarged the planet, then continued, "Yet, it was all barren – lacking the unique characteristics that varied the five beings from one another."

Twisting the wand downward, he discharged a crimson swirl into the center while furthering, "Decidedly so, the Red

Dracozim, Malguroz, began his work first. With his fires, he forged our lands and wrought the magma that would propel the earth around our sun through each of its ninety-one day seasons." Extracting the red tail outward, he maneuvered it in a circular motion to mold the mountains, islands, and valleys, then withdrew it back into the wand's tip as he left the globe engaged in a slow spin.

"Following the great scorches," uttered the Instructor as he discharged a pale mist that enveloped the earth, "Huregos, the Dracozim of White, unleashed a cooling breeze that calmed the flames and gave the finishing touches to the various land regions." After extracting most of the shroud, he brought the magical wand to his mouth. With an exhale that triggered his wand to fog outward, he remarked, "Then, he breathed out a nourishing air to safeguard the land from the lifeless space that surrounded it." As the white veil subsided, an atmosphere of clouds that floated in the sky was left behind.

With the students dazzled at the display, Instructor Pepperton slightly increased his fervor while flicking a sapphire-colored wave. Crashing it down onto the dry lands, he spouted, "Azuricar, the Blue Dracozim, followed with her gift that quenched the earth. She poured her essence into the far-reaching Endless Ocean and the smaller bodies throughout." Stirring the flow up from the southernmost landmark to the northern tip, the teacher energetically carried it outward onto the mountains while continuing, "Next, she reached out to the colder, elevated regions and crystallized her magic into an enveloping ice and snow." Zipping the streak onto the orbiting satellites, he concluded before withdrawing the blue wave, "Lastly, she imbued the two moons with her power to provide a rising and setting tide."

Noticing the students that gazed up in wonder alongside those who now began to gradually ascend off their padded seats, the energetic storyteller smiled. Although he delighted in their astonishment, Instructor Pepperton tried to bring the rising children back to their blanketed mats by lowering his spirited movement with a slowly drawn out, jade-colored sprinkle. As it fell, he released a few others at a faster pace that began to spread around the earth.

"The Green Dracozim, Geszia," he stated as the last droplet splattered and expanded in different directions, "sought to cultivate our environment by scattering enriched soil and minerals as nature was her gift." Lightly waving his wand, he moved the emerald sprouts upward from the dirt and continued, "Through this mixture, she flourished our terrain with vast grasslands, thick forests, and blossoming vegetation."

After hovering his instrument from the Emerald Forest to Deepwood, and all around, he retracted the green beams. Dimming the light that emanated from his wand, Instructor Pepperton focused on the students from right to left as he went on, "The world, as we have grown to know it, had taken its shape – one that pleased the divine race."

Shining a gold, glowing rim around the world, he said, "Lastly, the Yellow Dracozim, Deol, chose to give us the greatest gift of all and that which brings us here – life. Being selfless with his power, he desired to create all forms of existence in a way that would not only represent him, but embody the unique resemblance of his fellow gods. And so, he initiated the Dawning Age – devising a plan to craft from the most primal of creatures to the intellectual beings that would govern them."

Harnessing the surrounding light into a single orb, the Instructor carefully placed it over the world, then began to let loose small streaks of red, white, blue, and green towards it. While controlling the display, he continued, "Deol's intentions were pure, yet he was wisely cautious as he began to adopt magic that was unfamiliar to his aspect. Despite the calculated uncertainty, he pressed on – pouring his own harmonious thoughts of balance into the raw power."

Spouting several seedlings of only three colors into the lands, Instructor Pepperton went on, "Peaceful aquatic inhabitants that would make their homes within Azuricar's waters took shape, followed by woodland animals and flighted birds that took from Geszia and Huregos' design."

Discharging the final, red tail, Instructor Pepperton switched to a careful tone while explaining, "Volatile were the flames of Malguroz, but with Deol's design towards a state of equilibrium, they produced somewhat stable breeds – from beetles and wyrms, to hulking red and brown orcs, and the enormous, fire-breathing dragons we are all familiar with."

Exciting his audience once more, the Instructor painted the roaming orcs that were nearly six feet tall with his magical sparks, then proportionally reduced the design to show the majestic dragons that spanned over a hundred feet as a comparison. Intricately, he formed the expanding wings, sharp claws, armored scales, and muscular tails, while even including a smell of brimstone that emanated from their fanged maws.

Now seeking to ease the awed children and laying to rest any potential fears, he clarified while withdrawing all except the glowing orb of light over the world. "Despite the wild and dangerous beings that challenged the balance, they all lived in harmony. Some were peaceful when in their isolation, others naturally serene in the open, but all lived together."

Focusing towards the heart of the earth, Instructor Pepperton lit up the glistening yellow beam once more as he went on, "While all was good and well, Deol sought to continue his creations…"

Suddenly stopping the radiant gleam, he expressed with a watchful manner, "Yet, in spite of his desires, he halted after realizing an odd presence – an unforeseen result. A wild magic had been birthed among the stars, one sapped from the power of each divine being that formed itself into a new aspect of a black and silver hue."

Stirring his audience with a grey sphere that now sat alongside the gold one, he announced cautiously, "This sixth Dracozim soon made its presence known to all, proclaiming himself as Zolgaz." Shooting out the four elemental colors of red, white, blue, and green, the Instructor went on amid the children's gasps, "Noticed by all, this new being was welcomed – given safe haven among the heavens where the others resided."

Focusing deeper onto the silvery orb, he pointed out, "This newborn god soon witnessed a world teeming with life. Having seen the role each other had in its creation, the sixth grew a slight envy – craving to leave his own imprint, regardless of what his unknown essence may bring to the delicate balance." Taking the grey tail, he zipped it towards each other color while continuing, "Blindly seeking to shape a part of the land, the Grey Dracozim attempted to bargain with each individual aspect. To his frustration, he was turned down without hesitation by all except Deol as the others spoke of caution regarding potentially volatile repercussions."

Leaving the grey and yellow sparks as the center of attention, Instructor Pepperton carried on, "Sensing the growing impatience and irritation within the sixth aspect, the Yellow Dracozim approached with kindness and compassion. Deol, in his wisdom, attempted to counsel the new god –

suggesting the youthful one remain under his tutelage to learn of their divine powers and history."

Swirling the two orbs around one another with the golden one at the head, he went on, "For a time, Deol taught the newborn Dracozim of their purpose while maintaining his stance that creation had to be halted." Allowing the darker color to slowly overtake its lighter counterpart at the helm, he continued, "Yet, the sixth began to influence Deol over time as a subtle grief was noticed, one stemming from having paused creation just short of what was initially sought. Gradually, he manipulated the god of light by discussing how the four elemental Dracozim were allowed to finish their work, then speaking of his own grey essence as a blessing from life itself – one that must be used to fill the remaining void of what was left undone. Lastly, the deviant one bargained that he would channel his purity and order into any new beings to maintain the existing balance – a lie told to the kind god as only resentment and animosity were building within the newborn entity towards the ones he felt denied his birthright."

Dimming the golden essence, the Instructor focused solely on the silvery streak while moving on in a grim tone, "And so, the deceit had been done and creation renewed in spite of the unhindered warnings from the others. At first, Deol's initial hesitancy was replaced with a grand power when the obscure grey magic was tapped into."

Firing off dark shards with the tinted colors of the other elements, he continued, "More aggressive variations of existing animals were birthed at the start, soon followed by monstrous beasts." Brushing his wand along the world, Instructor Pepperton shaped it all – from the vicious timberwolves, giants, and yeti, to the rock-formed golems, corrupted orcs, and cyclopean creatures. After springing to life an animated ogre, he then wrought the flame drakes that were half the size of their dragon counterparts with twice the ferocity. As the students gasped, he added in a deeper voice, "And lastly, of pure darkness, spiritual manifestations that were spawned from the malice and jealousy within the Grey aspect's heart."

Having drawn the wild, mysterious entities to hang over remote regions, the children now grew frightened as some even closed their eyes. Yet, they were quickly calmed by a soothing light that Instructor Pepperton shone. Ending the dramatic portion of his presentation, he said in a softer voice while shining the light brighter by the second, "Although the Grey Dracozim had feigned his true intentions, Deol was able to relinquish this dark magic's veil before it was too late."

Now illuminating each and every child in the room, Instructor Pepperton remarked, "Responding with peace and wisdom, the Yellow Dracozim sought to strengthen the balance of life through that which was born of his sole essence. It is in you, in me, and all those in our peaceful lands that were given the most precious ability of all – to be able to wield the very magic the gods poured into this earth and the intelligence to understand it."

Stepping forward, he continued, "It was through the elves that Deol poured his greater discipline and intellect in the arcane. Granted immortal life spans, they were tasked with overseeing the sanctuary of others."

While some of the children grew disheartened as they were all humans within the room, Instructor Pepperton lifted them up with a smile and a more passionate tone while stating, "But the elves were few in number and lacked much of the disposition given to humanity. You see, our race was given Deol's very own creativity and resolve. We may be mortal, but our will grants us the greatest potential of all – to explore, to innovate, and to truly shape the balance of our world."

"Though," he warned, "we must not squander these gifts and stray from our call. We are responsible for the safekeeping of not only the lands within the Golden Realm, but across all of Erdaris itself."

Retracting the light that shone bright in the room, Instructor Pepperton lit the wand to his face while initiating his closing, "And with Deol's final labor, the Dracozim decreed a close to their work as they were all in need of regeneration after expending so much of their power during creation's course. Despite the unexpected results they encountered, they looked upon their world that was teeming with life with great joy and pleasure as they were no longer alone in the universe."

Whipping his wand one last time, he released four colored dragons of fire, air, water, and earth, then lowered them to the world while finishing, "So much was their satisfaction that throughout the centuries, the four elemental Dracozim chose to join us through shapeshifting avatars. Primarily disguised as great, winged beings, they settled where their powers were thickest – molten volcanoes, thundering peaks, oceanic trenches, and verdant forests."

Drawing all of the light back into his wand, except one small yellow orb, Instructor Pepperton concluded, "While these four chose to walk among the world, Deol decided to remain in the heavens – providing spiritual guidance and overseeing the balance of all."

Using another odd word of magic not known to the rest, the Instructor pulled back the blinds and ended his elaborate show. Before he could even utter another phrase, the captivated children let loose a slew of questions regarding the world, magic, and the dragons.

"In time, students," responded the teacher. "Although, we will not be riding them, we will meet them during our curriculum along with the elders who bound them. As to magic and more stories," he alternated, "we have our entire school year dedicated to learning more. We shall delve further into our history, our nation's birth, and how magic was harnessed."

"And the spells?" asked one child.

"When can we use them?" added another.

Attaching the wand back onto his belt, the calm Instructor answered, "All in its due course. Throughout your studies within The School, you shall learn magic's language, how to channel spells, but more importantly... the grand responsibilities that come with it.

"Now," the teacher motioned, "I ask you all to rise." As the students stood, he went on, "We shall take a short recess for those of you that may require use of the facilities, after which we shall rejoin for the remainder of this morning's schedule."

CHAPTER FIVE:

"SAVORING THE SWEET"

With each passing lesson and day of class, Cora came home with more excitement and joy than the last. Having now succeeded in the first month of her studies, she grew exceptionally elated that afternoon, so much so that her parents were barely able to get a word out during their walk back through the northeast housing section.

"And we even got to see a riding dragon today from the window," exclaimed Cora. "It's got great big wings, and it's so fast, and..."

As Cora ranted on, her mother only stared at her with a kind, attentive gaze. Yet, her father was mildly distracted – looking around towards the nearby merchants who displayed their wares.

Slowing his pace while turning to his child, Cehdric offered, "How's about a treat or two this afternoon?" Catching the attention of his daughter and wife who both came to a halt, he continued, "To celebrate your first month in the magical, gilded school."

"It's just 'The School', Poppa," corrected Cora with a slight smirk.

"My apologies, tulip," said Cehdric as he reacted with a chuckle.

"She's learning so much already," commented Aeyra after a brief laugh. "She'll be teaching us before we know it."

While they all shared a moment of joy, Cehdric looked through his pockets and pouches – but turned up with empty hands lined with threads of lint. Looking to his wife, he shook his head, forcing her to do the same and pluck up only a solitary, copper coin.

Growing disheartened, the two adults looked to one another, but were called towards their child as Cora mentioned, "It's alright, Momma. Poppa. I don't…"

Although her daughter still had words she wanted to say, Aeyra stepped in and affirmed, "Our little flower deserves a reward after how well she's done in class. We're just so proud of you."

"Aye," added her father, "even if it's just a small bite, a smidge. We love you and we'd give all we have to show it." Noticing her daughter's caring, selfless stance, he furthered, "At least, let us do this for you today."

"Please?" begged Aeyra. "For us?"

Despite her initial hesitancy, Cora agreed with her parents as it was a request that would make them happy. With her nod, they all joined hands and went down the aisle of nearby merchants – perusing their stock.

First, Cora set her eyes on a large, sweet cake of honey and almonds, but moved away from it as the request was several silver from the bellowing vendor. Next, she saw a delectable golden apple that was coated in an amber caramel upon the next stall. Yet, it was quite a few pieces of copper – so she once again shied away without a word.

Noticing the considerate attitude of their daughter who avoided any costly items despite her appetite's desire, Cehdric said, "What about these, tulip?" Pointing to a nearby booth with several candied fruits shaped into flowers and birds, he went on, "You love berries and honey."

"Yes," commented Aeyra who joined in to hand her husband the coin, "we'll get you one."

Overhearing the nearby family, the High Elven merchant who attended the stand addressed, "Greetings, may I assist you with one of our assorted delights?"

Moving past the brittle and pecans, then over to the display of hardened honey that held a fruit-filled center, Cehdric responded, "Greetings to you as well. We're here with our daughter who just completed her first month at 'The School'."

Looking over to Cora, he winked. After returning the same expression, Cora smiled with joy – content with her father's efforts.

As the elf stood idly by with a feigned interest in the reason for their visit, Cehdric continued, "We'd like to purchase the dove and rose shaped ones, if we may."

"Excellent choice," uttered the elf. "They shall be two copper coins."

Peering down to his daughter, Cehdric apologetically said, "Seems we're only able to just get you the one. Which do you prefer?"

While the child made her selection, the father offered up the lone copper coin, but was rejected as the vain shopkeeper proudly stated, "Two copper, each."

"Please," begged Cehdric, "could you just…"

"No," interrupted the High Elf.

"What if we offer our gardening services at your home?" asked Cehdric. "We can…"

"Once more, no," interjected the merchant. "Perhaps in Arulan you may barter services. However, if you do not have the coin here, then you had best be on your way."

Abruptly and with a rude expression, the elven vendor turned around and walked away from the family. With Cora and Cehdric heartbroken, Aeyra began to pace inward as the proud matriarch that she was. Her face was blushed and in clear anger, one not usually seen by the two.

"Please, can we go home, Momma?" requested Cora as her father began to talk her mother out of any action.

"In a moment, honey," remarked Aeyra, who was clearly furious with the way her family was talked down to. "That's no way to speak to us."

Just as she shook off her husband's hold, Aeyra was caught off guard by another voice who spoke from behind them, "I very much agree, there is no excuse to be impolite to a kind family from Arulan."

As the Everstone family turned, they saw a merchant who had wandered from his booth and stepped towards them. Being the first to react, Aeyra clarified, "We're citizens of the Golden Realm, just like you."

"I meant no offense," said the friendlier High Elf. After a light bow of his head, he continued, "It is simply the accent. As you are also a human family, it is an assumption – an honest mistake if you would allow my error."

"I… forgive me as well," remarked the mother as she turned to a calmer state. Introducing her family as a way of amending her actions, she continued, "I'm Aeyra, this is my husband Cehdric, and our daughter, Cora. We're from Riverbend."

"A fine family from a delightful town near Arulan's farms," returned the kind elven vendor. "The bottommost fork of the Elarun River, if I am correct?" As the two parents nodded, he furthered, "I am Hawlon Honeydew, if it pleases you." Signaling them towards his stall, he went on, "By way of apologies on behalf of Taylik, please come with me. Most of us on this merchant's row are unlike him. His wares may be sweet, yet his mood is far from it."

Showing their gratitude, the family smiled and thanked the elven attendant. While making their way to his humble stand, Hawlon inquired, "What brings you to our shops this fine afternoon?"

"Our daughter's just finished her first month at 'The School'," responded Aeyra. "We want to celebrate with a small treat for her."

"Ah," uttered the merchant, "a future magister." Turning back towards the child as he reached his booth, he furthered, "A great one in the making, I am certain." Standing tall behind his display, he finished, "You must be quite proud."

"We truly are," answered Aeyra as both she and Cehdric passionately nodded.

"Good marks I presume?" asked Hawlon.

As all looked towards Cora for an answer, she said, "Well, umm... we haven't had any tests yet, but I've been studying."

"She's been receiving compliments for her good behavior and generosity," boasted Aeyra.

"And making new friends," chimed in Cehdric.

"It is an honor then to serve such an esteemed student," complimented Hawlon towards Cora. "Go on," he said. "Choose any delight from my store so that you may take home with you."

Pointing towards an array of sweets and savory treats, Hawlon exhibited each – from his pies and cakes, to his candies and tarts. Yet, Cora did not look at any of the larger or more elaborate items. Instead, she focused on a single drop of taffy. While she asked politely for the coin her father held, the kind merchant interjected.

"Are you certain that is all for today, my lady?" asked Hawlon while offering a slew of fancy delights that were each refused by the considerate child.

"Please, just that one," responded Cora while extending her arm with the copper coin.

"I am afraid, that will not do," remarked the vendor. Grabbing a small bag made of waxed parchment and his wooden scoop, he picked up several pieces of taffy. After filling it to the brim, he handed it towards her while saying, "Now this is a treat for a young magister."

Although Cora continued her attempts to give the coin, Hawlon did not take it. Rather, he grabbed two more delights from his store – a pair of sticks with hardened honey and caramel swirls. As he handed the sweets to the parents, Aeyra stepped in.

"Thank you, but we mustn't," remarked the mother.

"All we have is the one copper," added the father.

Not mindful of the items and their cost, Hawlon insisted, "Today is a day of celebration, money should not be on your mind – only the accomplishments of your wonderful daughter."

Although they held the items handed to them by the merchant, the Everstone family was still hesitant to take them. They offered payment from their future wages and even gardening services, yet all were denied.

Leaning in towards them, Hawlon furthered, "You have all worked hard enough in just your first month here at the Golden Citadel, I am afraid I must continue to insist." In a lower tone, he went on towards the mother and father, "I have also seen the work you both have achieved within the northern gardens in such a short time – the two strangers who came in to tidy the displays. Wondrous and elegant they have become."

"It's mostly her," mentioned Cehdric. "She's the real caretaker, I just follow what she tells me."

"It's both of us," amended Aeyra.

"And we are thankful to have each of you here among us," concluded Hawlon with a bow of his head.

For a short time, the three elders exchanged their praise and stories, all while Cora stood by. At first, she smiled and nodded to the words, then she stuck her hand into the bag of sweets. Pulling out a piece of taffy that was dried on the outside, she stuck it in her mouth. While her parents continued to talk, she mashed into the chewy candy – struggling with her small teeth at the beginning, then enjoying the elastic treat that continuously released its honey flavor with each bite.

Joyous was their afternoon encounter, but it was now under threat of interruption by a far off, low boom of thunder that paused their actions.

"Seems we have a mild storm brewing," commented Hawlon as he stared into the distant east. "Hope it does not hamper the festival's preparation."

"Festival?" asked Cehdric. "For the day of remembrance?"

"For the Jubilee of the Four Stars, yes," responded Hawlon. "We have a far grander affair here at the capital than any other town or even nation."

Interjecting between the two after staring at the dark clouds, Aeyra said, "I'm certain we'll see you there, yet we'd best head back home." Looking at her daughter who continued to chomp on her treat, she went on, "To keep dry and get to bed early for tomorrow's class."

"Yes'h, Momma," mumbled Cora with a smile full of sugary morsels.

As another crack of thunder roared in the faraway east, several of the nearby merchants began putting away their wares, covering their stalls with large canvases, and closing their shops. Though the storm was not near, all around reacted to the coming rain.

"I ask you please excuse me while I secure my stand," requested Hawlon. "It seems I must also part ways for now."

Despite going on that he did not require any assistance, Cehdric still offered his services. "Let me help you while my wife takes our little magister home," he said. "It's the very least we could do."

Sensing the father would persist as he was denied the ability to repay the savory delights, Hawlon reluctantly agreed.

While the two went about the labor of sealing the small store, Aeyra took her daughter by the hand. Both mother and child pecked their father on the cheek with a gentle kiss, then bid their final thanks to the kind merchant.

After their farewell, Cora clutched her mother as both made their way through the stony streets and back to their humble cottage within the northeastern section.

CHAPTER SIX:

"GUESTS OF THE STREAM"

P attering on the roof, a steady stream of droplets trickled its way down the shingles – creating a curtain in front of the westward kitchen window. Calmly, a golden-haired child sat near the display brought about by the soothing rain as a pair of steps echoed behind her.

Approaching somewhat slowly, her mother stepped in from behind and said in a low voice, "Cora, honey, it's getting late."

Although the child acknowledged, Aeyra leaned in close and landed her elbows onto the counter where her daughter had set herself on. "This one's soft, peaceful," she remarked while also looking outward to the storm.

As Cora turned to face her mother, Aeyra continued, "I'll be with you while it passes."

Delicately landing a kiss atop her daughter's head, the mother lastly asked, "Let's get ready for bed, shall we?"

Thrusting her head up and down, Cora nodded and let out a light yawn, then responded, "Yes, Momma."

Moving upward from her seated position, Cora revealed the bag of honey taffy that was mostly full, sparking her mother to ask, "Saving the treats for another day?"

With a grin, Cora answered, "For tomorrow. To share with the class, Momma."

Proud of her child's considerate heart and mind, Aeyra returned the smile and said, "I'm certain your friends will be delighted." Lifting herself up, she continued, "Poppa and I will make sure they're packed in the morning." Bellowing to the small, front room to her left, she finished, "Won't we?"

Hearing his wife, Cehdric relinquished his hold on the boots he was cleaning and sat up. "Of course," he instinctively agreed without question. Taking a step forward, he inquired, "Off to bed?"

"Yes," confirmed Aeyra. "Don't wait up for me tonight."

Walking through the adjoining room, Cehdric did not utter a word until he kissed his wife. As he pulled back, he said, "You take care of her." Plucking Cora's hand upward and pecking it softly with his lips, he continued towards his daughter, "Of Momma. Tuck her in and make sure she rests, understood?"

While her father leaned down and smirked, Cora responded, "Yes, Poppa."

"Thank you, tulip," returned Cehdric.

Although she desired more time together as a family, Aeyra caressed her daughter and pulled her inward due to the late hour. Before her farewell to her husband, she asked, "Sharpen the shears we used today if you can. They're a bit dull."

"Certainly," acknowledged the father after sharing one last gentle kiss with his beloved.

Partaking in the moment, Cora embraced her father's waist, but was interrupted as her mother said, "Come along, honey."

Turning her daughter around, Aeyra led her right through the kitchen and into the narrow hall, then towards the door directly across where they dined. Pushing open the creaking entrance, Aeyra revealed the smaller room that held a modest rocking chair and a table of oak. Moving past the two pieces, she went to the corner where a chamber pot and a bowl of water atop a stand awaited.

Looking to her child, the dutiful mother remarked, "Let's clean that sugar off your fingers before bed."

Clearly growing more tired by the moment, Cora joined her mother's side in front of the water-filled dish without a word. As her hands were washed, she let out a heavy blink, followed by a light yawn. Distracted by her tired mood, Cora impulsively brought her soaked hands to her dress, but was halted by her mother.

"Let's use a towel," said Aeyra – directing her child to wipe her digits on the cotton cloth rather than her nightly attire.

With her hands dried, Cora walked to her bed, then sat atop the straw-filled mattress. Positioning herself back, she adjusted her body to the edge of the covers, then allowed her mother to bring the blanket over her slender frame.

Having tucked in her daughter, Aeyra asked, "A story tonight?"

As Cora replied only with a longer, more drawn out yawn than before, Aeyra responded, "Sleep it is, then." After a peck on her forehead, she checked the sheets to ensure all was sound and in place, then took a seat at the chair next to her daughter.

For the first few moments, the dutiful mother was watchful, but began to lower her guard and feel at ease as her child lay comfortably on her side – only turning once to face the room's east window.

While the time passed, Aeyra began to yawn and look in the same direction where the gentle rain splashed onto the small, outer shutters. Slowly, she grew mesmerized – listening to the peaceful, soothing tune of each drop as it rang onto the tiny frame. Before she knew it, she began to fade into sleep as her daughter had done before her.

Several hours passed as midnight faded into the dark hours that immediately followed it. As the storm picked up in pace, the once harmonious melody turned into a deeper downpour. Awoken by the louder sounds, Aeyra shuddered her eyes, then stood up in a mildly groggy state.

First, she checked her child – ensuring she was still safe and asleep. Next, she looked to the window that began to slightly tremble from the steady breeze that brought the resounding rain. Going over to the sill, she fastened the twin latches – digging them deeply into the ledge, but releasing several droplets of water that had built up between the gaps.

Before she could look at the rest of the wooden frame, Aeyra heard her daughter.

"Momma?" asked Cora.

"It's alright, honey," she answered. "It's locked now, we can both go back to bed."

Despite her tired state, Cora kept her eyes on her mother – watching as she sat back in her chair to continue resting.

Following her elder's example, the young child turned back towards the window she faced. First, she silently rearranged herself – moving away from the recently moistened patch of her blanket that she had touched. Then, she resumed her motionless state while watching the drops of rain that battered onto the hazy glass.

In only a few passing seconds, Cora's eyes grew heavy. The once fast paced droplets she witnessed now seemed to relinquish their speed in favor of keeping up with the bat of her lashes. Yet, she paid no mind to the sluggish drops that now appeared to stand still in the air with her last blink. A trick, she presumed, one played by the mind before sleep fully takes hold.

With her eyes shut and her thoughts relaxed, only the sound seemed to remain – a lazy splash, one that soon faded into silence.

As all was quiet, a loud crash of water echoed around her and startled her awake. Forcing herself up, she now saw the dark, stormy night was gone – replaced by the clear light of day that passed through a clouded sky.

Staring up in disbelief while now on her feet, Cora remained still at first, but then began to move as she noticed the same resounding splash of water behind her. With a quick turn, she confirmed the source of its noise – an armored soldier who knelt atop a bed of plush grass by a steadily-flowing stream.

Silently, Cora watched as his pulled-back, dark brown hair and long, elven ears dragged down while he brought handfuls of water to his parched face. With each motion, he breathed out a heavy pant that seemed to hint of exhaustion.

While the warrior only gave attention to the stream's flow, Cora could not help but glance at the items near his side – a pair of dirty gauntlets, a stained leaf-bladed sword, and a damaged helmet painted in mostly gold with dulled silver accents. Hints of a harsh battle were upon all of the pieces, a sight Cora tried to distance herself from as she shook her

53

head and cowered backwards while raising her hands to her face.

Her eyes were shut, her head was kept low as she started to repeatedly whisper, "I'll wake up soon, I'll wake up soon."

As if she were expecting some event to take her back home, Cora kept reopening her eyes, then scrunching them harder with each new attempt.

"Please," she began to beg, "you haven't let me help before. I don't know what to do. Just let me go home before the scary bird comes."

Despite her efforts, Cora was unable to draw a single word from the soldier. Instead, the elven combatant only reached for another handful of water, but this time bringing it towards one of his wounds – a sight that caused the frightened child to tremble and duck.

Acting as if she once again knew what was to come, Cora covered her ears. But, it did not seem to matter since the piercing cry of a slow-flying vulture from high above rattled her nonetheless. Now diving aggressively towards her position, Cora let out a scream that forced her to accidentally sidestep into the nearby stream.

"Momma!" she called in a frightful panic. "I-it came again. Momma, the…"

Before she finished her sentence, Cora opened her eyes and noticed what she had been expecting did not happen. Instead of a fading dream that would throw her back into her bed, she remained stuck in the flowing waters – watching helplessly as the threatening bird circled about before flying off to the northwest after another hissing shriek.

Unsure of what to now expect as each passing second was new to her, Cora started to breathe rapidly. "Please," she began again towards the soldier in a distressful manner, "help me. I need to go home."

Hoping her efforts were not in vain, Cora once more repeated while tears formed in her eyes, "Please."

"Hmm," nodded the elf who at long last seemed to listen.

Raising himself up and staring outward with his emerald eyes, the High Elven warrior continued, "It may be too late for me, but it is not for you. We shall get you home."

Wiping her eyes and growing a smile of relief, Cora opened her mouth to speak, but was silenced as another spoke before her words came out.

"I will not run from the northern legions," said a stalwart, female voice from behind Cora.

Quickly, the startled child turned to face the other elf. As her body swept around, Cora could not help but let out a light gasp towards what seemed to be a familiar face.

"M-miss, Head Instructor?" mumbled the confused Cora as she stared towards what seemed to be the Arch Magister of her school, but one without the noticeable signs of aging she was accustomed to seeing.

As Cora tried to gain the attention of the Head Instructor, she was interrupted by the male warrior who shouted, "No."

Setting his focus solely towards his fellow soldier, he continued, "Try not to move, Astrael." Dashing over the small stream, he ignored all else and ran right through Cora as if she were a shadow, then right into the falling arms of the female elf.

In disbelief, Cora looked around herself and grew into a deeper state of shock. She realized that no one saw her, heard her, and nothing affected her as even the water seemed to pass unhindered between her feet when she looked down. Although she had fallen into the stream, not a single part of her, even her night dress, was wet or dripping.

Astonished and now feeling overwhelmed, Cora could only stand idly by as the two High Elves spoke to one another.

"You must go," uttered Astrael as she coughed heavily and raised her bloodied, left arm to the male elf's shoulder.

At first, he did not respond, the warrior only tore off a piece of his exposed shirt to bandage Astrael's hand and forearm.

"It will scar and the darkness may spread," he said while finishing the dressing, "but it shall begin to heal with time."

"High General, my lord," Astrael interrupted, "do not worry over me. I am able to stay and fight with the others. You need to get to safety."

"No," replied the valiant male elf, "I will not let the enemy splinter and risk endangering any innocent village or others around us. Since it seems I am as much the prize as what we carry, I must remain and see this through."

"But I am the only magister left, at least send another," bargained Astrael.

Standing up, the High General whistled first, then answered, "This is not up for discussion." As a handful of battered soldiers came from over the small hill in front of the stream, he continued, "You did well today, now you must endure for what is yet to come."

Looking over towards one of his approaching fellows, he questioned, "Is that bloody bird finally gone?"

"For now," answered the subordinate.

"But the rest are closing on us with haste," added another elf.

Shaking his head, the High General only whispered, "Time is against us." Now moving over to where a pair of large cloaks lay spread out behind Astrael, the commanding warrior pulled them out – revealing an injured horse that kept still until it was called to rise.

Struggling to lift itself up, the mare gave its best, but required the assistance of the rest to stand. Now upright, the High General removed all of the gold adornments and armor, only leaving the saddle on while offering a few kind words of encouragement to the hurt steed.

"Only a short ride," he said. "Then, you both can rest."

As the High General and the others turned to Astrael, she declined their assistance and limped on her own to the horse. With a few short steps, she had made it, but then realized she would be unable to climb on by herself. After a reluctant nod, her fellows quickly aided her up onto the saddle, then fastened her feet into the stirrups.

Coming to her side as the others stepped back, the High General said, "Straight to Brightfork."

Acknowledging the order, Astrael only sluggishly bobbed her head down, then up. As she looked to the High General, she reached down with her bandaged forearm and said, "At least make yourself presentable, for when the rest arrive."

Leaning further inward, Astrael used the back of her hand where it was cleanest to brush the deeply smudged pin that hid her superior's rank. With a few quick motions, she first focused on the surrounding five-headed dragon, but did so in a distracting manner that allowed her to simultaneously and without notice reach into her side satchel with the other arm. Next, she moved onto the crossed red sword and blue hammer at the badge's center as she plucked the crimson gem from the broken bits of her bagged wand. Lastly, she touched on the green arrow that joined the alliance symbol down the middle while withdrawing her right hand out of the pouch.

"There you are," she said after finishing her few seconds of work.

As the High General offered a thankful, yet hasty expression, Astrael added, "Wait."

With the last of her might and speed, Astrael shoved her right hand towards her commander's pin, uttering the words, "Berchigo."

Instinctively, the High General took a step back from the unexpected action – helplessly observing as Astrael collapsed while a warm red glow set itself on his left shoulder. The glare was bright for a moment, then quickly subsided after providing a soothing hum from the gem that was now latched onto his pin.

Despite its delayed comfort, all those around the commanding elf were startled – particularly the unnerved Cora who still observed the sight and the ailing horse.

Clearly being the most distraught from the flash, the steed began to rile itself up with each passing second. First it neighed, then it circled about with the motionless Astrael who had fainted atop its back.

Worried about limiting the horse's reaction to their side of the hill, the surrounding High Elves cautiously attempted to restrain it, but did so carefully at first as they feared injuring it further. Only when the beast began to cross into the stream's shallow waters and kick upwards, did their motions become more intense.

Yet, their containment began to fail, so the High General selflessly stepped forward from the rest – lunging between the horse's hooves to grab the reins. Tugging the leather strap downward, he pointed the horse to the south, then shouted, "Go!"

Obeying the command, the horse scurried off as it was bid, but not before kicking off one last time from the shallow stream. In its excited state, the steed sent forth a large wave of water towards Cora's direction – one causing her to impulsively crouch and hide from, despite her not being affected by her surroundings. But to her surprise, this rush seemed different as she was able to feel the initial spray, then the main body of its splash as it struck her head on.

Dripping from her hair to her feet, Cora lifted herself up and tried to get the attention of the elves around her by crying out, "Help me, please."

At first, all she heard was silence, then the creak of wood as it rocked back, then forth, followed by the footsteps of a rushing body. The slender, yet firm hands of the approaching person wrapped around her soaked, cold body. Being held tightly, Cora was barely able to move, but felt comforted as the hands brushed her drooping, wet hair that hung over her closed eyes.

Slowly, Cora bat her lashes once and saw a dark figure. Before being forced to close them once more due to the dripping water, she said, "Please, I just want to go home."

"Cora, honey," replied the familiar, warm voice of her mother. "I'm here, you're home safe."

Without a moment's hesitation, the distressed child began to cry, prompting Aeyra to reiterate as a protective matriarch, "I'm here. I'm here."

As she cradled her daughter, Aeyra grew increasingly concerned with how her daughter became drenched in water while sleeping in bed. Her first instinct was to check the latches and the window frame with one free hand, but verified they were secure. Now looking up, she confirmed that there were no dripping cracks from the ceiling either.

Baffled, Aeyra decided to peer outside. As she unfastened the panes to move the shutters that had been thrown over the hazy glass by the wind, she let out an apprehensive gasp. While still holding Cora, the mother became speechless as she stared in disbelief at the alarming sight of each and every raindrop around her house being suspended in midair – appearing as if they were frozen in time.

CHAPTER SEVEN:

"A DREAM'S TALE"

With a pound and a thrash, the wooden front door of the Everstone home rattled. Once, then twice, and continuously it thumped until the family responded to its sound.

"Cehdric!" shouted the perturbed mother from Cora's room. "See who it is already!"

Dashing to the forward room of the house, the disconcerted husband pressed to the oval door, then pulled it to reveal a dark silhouette that was blotted mostly by the morning sun's glare.

As the figure moved into the dimly lit house with urgency, Cehdric responded, "We're late, Cora, all of us. We're sorry, it's just…"

Interrupting him, the hooded guest removed her cloak while asking, "Where is the child?"

As Cehdric stared at the Arch Magister, he tried to further apologize for Cora's absence, but was once more paused as she urged, "We have not much time, take me to her."

Acknowledging the request, the dutiful husband nodded and led The School's matriarch down the narrow hall, then to the final door on the right. As they entered the small bedroom, both saw the mother first, who cradled her distraught and softly crying daughter with a soothing melody and a gentle rocking. Concerned with his sobbing child, Cehdric gave no hesitation to looping around the Arch Magister and joining his wife's side.

Just as her husband had done, Aeyra began to apologize for their daughter's tardiness, but was hushed by an amiable gesture from the Arch Magister who continued to insist that was not her concern.

Gazing firmly upon the two parents who appeared equally as exhausted from the lack of rest, the elder magister pressed, "Tell me. What happened in the night?"

"Another nightmare," answered the mother while the father nodded in agreement.

"What did she see?" followed the Arch Magister.

While Aeyra looked down to caress her daughter, Cehdric simply pointed at the Head Instructor. "You," he said.

Nodding with a somber look, the Arch Magister peered down to Cora and addressed only her. "Miss Everstone, Cora," she said, "can you describe to me what you saw?"

Lifting her teary-eyed face up from her mother's embrace, Cora looked to the Head Instructor. After a sniffle and wipe of her nose, she bobbed her head up and down. "Y-you were hurt," she stuttered at first. "I tried, I couldn't do anything. It never lets me."

"What else?" prodded the Head Instructor after reassuring the parents and their child with a calm gesture.

"The scary bird," said Cora after brushing her eyes, "it kept staring. It came at me again, more times, but it left." Being encouraged by the Arch Magister to continue, Cora went on, "A horse was there, too."

"What was its condition, injured?" questioned the elder.

"Y-yes," answered Cora. "It was crying, laying down."

"And what else?" furthered the Arch Magister with intrigue.

"You were with it," said Cora. "You left on it after the flash."

"What color was this flash?" asked the High Elf.

"Red," responded Cora. "Bright."

"Hmm," uttered the Arch Magister as she moved herself back and pondered on what the child said.

With the Head Instructor taking a step away, Cora added, "I didn't know what to do, I just wanted to go home."

"And so you are," answered the elder elf. "You are here, safe with your family where you can recover your strength."

"B-but class," remarked Cora.

"Worry not," replied the Head Instructor. "It shall be there waiting for you tomorrow. Today, you rest without concern."

As Cora let out a somber smile, Aeyra lifted herself and called her husband to carry on the duty of being at their child's side. "Stay with Poppa for a moment," she said.

After gently kissing her daughter's forehead, Aeyra made her way to the room's door, then motioned for the Arch Magister to follow.

When they were far enough away in the hall, Aeyra asked in a concerned, somewhat harsh manner, "You said you'd help if we came. She's getting worse. Will she ever be done with these nightmares?"

"Please," said the Arch Magister in an attempt to calm the irritated mother, "we are doing all we can with what we know, and shall continue to do so."

"And what is it you know?" questioned Aeyra. "What's all this mean to you?"

"It is not a matter simply described to one not familiar with the arcane," answered the Arch Magister.

"This is my daughter we're speaking about," said the distressed mother. "Make me understand."

Sensing the tension from the worried parent, the Arch Magister attempted to calm her. "I meant you no offense," she said first. "Please, let us sit so I can do my best to clarify."

With a nod, the mother took a seat alongside the elf in the forward room and allowed her to continue. "Cora," said the magister, "is experiencing genuine visions – glimpses in time that have or could happen."

"She can see the future?" asked Aeyra.

"Not that we are aware of yet," responded the Arch Magister. "However, she has seen the past."

"How do you know?" begged the mother.

"Because I was there," explained the elder. "What she has described, I can now fully confirm since I witnessed this firsthand over nine centuries ago." As the mother listened with interest, she went on, "Cora, just as any other human, is far too young to have lived through it and what she sees is not mentioned in the historical books and songs – ones she still has not even covered in The School." Speaking softer, she continued, "She is experiencing what most of us recall as Baydyn's Gambit, where the High General of our armies set in motion the Battle at the Sunford Fields – the event that turned the tide to our favor during that devastating, twenty-four year war.

"My Cora?" said Aeyra. "In a battle?" Raising her voice, she continued, "She's an innocent child, you can't let her go back there."

"Rest assured," remarked the Arch Magister, "your child is not in any danger. It appears she can see what is happening, but cannot interact with or be harmed by it."

"But she was drenched," argued the mother. "She said she was in a stream."

"The evening's rain likely," clarified the Arch Magister. "Coupled with the upcoming anniversary of the war's end, it could explain why she continues to experience these glimpses that strengthen as she grows."

"We kept her dry at night, before bed," uttered Aeyra. "We've seen what happens when she's around so much water."

"As you and your husband often refer to your child, she is a flower," said the Arch Magister. "She will need to nourish so that she may bloom, and water is that which she requires. Her magic is tied to each drop surrounding her, from the largest pool to the tiniest spray, and every sip she takes of it. You cannot expect to withdraw her from it completely, less she wither." Placing her hand atop the mother's, she continued, "Her gifts, her visions, are unique; ones rare for elves in these times of late, and a far greater rarity among humans. What she possesses in the arcane will find its way to show itself, which is precisely why we all need to understand it better so she can be taught to control it."

"So it's a curse she must learn to deal with?" asked Aeyra who pulled her hand back to wipe a tear that lingered on her eyelid.

"Rather a responsibility she has been given," said the patient instructor. "She is blessed with a natural talent, one superior to most of her current peers. So, I ask you – allow us to teach her as one of advanced skill, among the classes given solely to the High Elves. All so that she may flourish."

"Will she be ready for such a leap?" questioned the mother.

"It will be a challenge, yet with all of us there for her, she shall be," comforted the Arch Magister. "This curriculum will allow us to expedite her magical learning so she can command her gift, rather than let it have charge over her. And," offered the thoughtful elf, "I will personally see to her care within The School. It is the very least I can do for a compassionate student who has shown such kindness, generosity, and willingness to learn in just the short amount of time she has been with us."

"She'll be saddened to be away from her friends," said Aeyra while lowering her head in thought. "But she'll be excited to meet new ones."

"And she shall be around all – old and new – within The School," assured the Arch Magister.

"Then," said the mother while raising her head, "Cehdric and I'd agree to her advancement, and I'm certain Cora would also."

Now sharing a smile with the mother, the Arch Magister said, "We are delighted to…"

Before the Head Instructor could finish her thoughts, the front door of the humble home flung open. After the initial crash and boom, the sound of metal clanking atop the floor's wooden planks resounded throughout the walls as two Highguards with pikes entered first, followed by a pair with horned longbows, and a final set with sword and shield. At a disciplined pace, they crossed into the forward room in a tight formation, then split in half – allowing a large opening at their center. As they settled, the elven guards shifted their weapons to rest just in front of them and shared no word while staring forward without acknowledgement for those they intruded upon.

Having caught the attention of all within the house, Cehdric peered out the room while Cora stood just behind – peeking out only slightly, but hiding most of her body. As they all stared at the unannounced marching within their cottage, a tall shadow loomed by the doorway. Taking a step inward, the figure paused, then resumed after adjusting its robed sleeves in a pompous manner.

Being the first to approach the looming guest, the Head Instructor reacted by standing up and saying, "Davik, you are…"

Countering the words as if irritated, the intruding male elf interjected with a cold-eyed stare, "Right on time, it would seem." In an arrogant but formal voice, he continued, "And is that any manner to announce the head of your order?"

Waving his hand as if perturbed with the lighting, the male elf signaled a set of guards – forcing one to open the westward blinds that were shut, and another to the east.

As the light shone onto the commanding elf's impeccable complexion, he went on while circling his head around the furnishings of the home, "These lodgings, so quaint. Such a simplistic design when compared to the rest." After making his arrogant comments known, he looked to the Head Instructor that appeared far older than him and said, "You care not to introduce me?"

Letting out a visible sigh, the perturbed Astrael said, "As you wish, my lord." Turning to the family, she continued, "This is Grand Magister Davik Silverlocke."

Feeling as if the introduction was cut short, the uninvited elf added in a prideful manner, "Head of the Magisters' Order within the Grand Sanctum."

"But not of The School," uttered the Head Instructor in a lower tone while standing next to Aeyra.

Reacting to the barely heard comment, Davik said, "Would you care to speak up, Astrael?" While the Head Instructor remained in a silent frustration, he continued, "Very well, then."

While gazing around to all those in the home, Davik went on with the purpose for his intrusion. "So this is it," he said, "the home of the student who stopped the rain in this housing section." Particularly staring towards the rear of the hall where Cehdric and Cora stood, he asked, "Was it your older sibling, child?"

Moving past the side of the Head Instructor, Aeyra motioned towards the hall – attracting the attention of the armed guards. As she halted in a brief fright, the Grand Magister flicked his hand and allowed her to keep moving towards the rear rooms.

Joining the side of her husband, the mother and father now grabbed their child's hand. Being bashful at first, Cora shook her head, but then took a step forward with the kind encouragement offered by her parents.

"This is our daughter, Cora," said the mother. "Our eldest and only child."

"She is the source?" questioned Davik. "But she is so small, so young."

Turning towards the family, Astrael answered before any other. "Miss Everstone," she said, "is a gifted pupil."

"Well then," thought Davik, "I can see why you have taken such an interest in arriving here personally, rather than sending an envoy of The School to check on your absent student. It appears to be a similar interest shared by the Order's Council." Setting his light blue eyes upon Cora, he continued, "Come closer, child."

First, Cora looked to her mother, then her father. As both shared a nod, she stepped forward while both parents remained just behind. Walking towards the Grand Magister, her eyes were only briefly caught by the single-headed dragon pin the two guards in front of her wore.

"Have you seen that mark before?" asked Davik as he noticed the child's action.

"Y-yes," stumbled Cora. "But it had more dragons."

"How many more did you count?" inquired Davik.

"Five," answered Cora.

"Interesting," thought the Grand Magister aloud while stroking his dimpled chin. Turning over to Astrael, he furthered, "Has her class visited the General at the Highguard Armory or the High King's Palace yet?"

"No," replied Astrael.

Continuing his stare onto his subordinate, Davik questioned, "And how long has this Arulonian family stayed among us in the Golden Citadel?"

"Just over a month," interjected Aeyra. "And we're not Arulonian, we're citizens just like you."

"From Riverbend," added Cehdric.

Staring high towards the ceiling as if offended by the uncalled remarks, Davik only resumed his gaze onto Astrael as he continued, "How does a child from a small farming village at our southern border know the insignia of a General, one she presumably has never met before?" Stepping once to look down upon the Arch Magister, he went on, "Either this is all chance or you have withheld information from me, proving my sources for these rumors have some truth, if not all."

After a disappointing look, Davik set his eyes down towards Cora, then said, "Tell me, child. Have you had visions – sights into the past, the future?"

69

Before Cora could answer, Astrael stepped in and said, "We only just confirmed its validity, she has."

"Of?" asked the Grand Magister.

Hesitating at first, Astrael first looked to Cora with a comforting nod, then answered after returning to a neutral stare towards Davik, "Baydyn's Gambit."

"Quite interesting, a moment I recall as if it were yesterday," said Davik as his eyes appeared to light up. While signaling his guards, he continued, "Very well, escort just the child to her new quarters within the Grand Sanctum."

"You can't," lashed out the mother as several Highguards stepped forward.

While the two parents huddled protectively near their daughter, Astrael interrupted by pushing herself between the elves and the human family. "I concur with her parents," she said.

In a rude tone, Davik commented, "You presume to have authority over me?"

After a calming breath, Astrael replied, "I do not. However, the child must continue her training to be of use to the council."

"The human classes are wasted upon this child who shows so much promise," remarked Davik. "Her history lessons, her tours of our cities, it is all secondary."

"I am inclined to agree," said the Head Instructor. While Davik's interest was sparked, she continued, "Rather than seclude her with the council, I suggest an alternative – one where she can still advance rapidly, yet remain among her peers. A solution her parents have already agreed upon, to place her among the High Elf students."

In a condescending manner, Davik commented, "You would allow this human child to partake in the same curriculum as our most prized pupils, ones far older than her? This is rare, Astrael, even for you."

"I would," answered Astrael proudly. Looking towards the parents, then Cora with a brief smile, she continued, "Miss Everstone is more than capable of meeting every expectation. She is one of our brightest, most dedicated students."

Providing a judgmental look towards the Arch Magister, Davik said, "I shall personally hold you accountable for the child. Should she fail with your way, then we shall have no choice but to intervene and do as I propose." Pausing for a moment, he tilted his head upwards to gaze up at the ceiling. While shifting his stare to and from several wooden beams, he concluded, "For the good of the Golden Realm, of course."

Turning about, the Grand Magister flung his long, silvery blonde hair and golden garments. With a snap of his fingers, the Highguards then followed him outward into the morning sun while offering no farewell to the family and Arch Magister they left behind.

As the door shut behind the rude elves, the Head Instructor offered her apology. "I did not mean for any of this to happen," she said. "I must ask your forgiveness, Miss Everstone." Looking solely at the child, she went on, "Your parents and I believe in you. We know you are up for the task, but can you prove it to everyone else?"

Under the continued encouragement of her parents, Cora shook her head up and down, then said, "Yes, Miss Head Instructor."

Visibly, both Aeyra and Cehdric followed by expressing their happiness towards the Arch Magister that asked for their daughter's sentiment. "May we offer you tea?" they asked.

With a regretful look, the Arch Magister replied, "I must unfortunately decline as I have several preparations to make for Miss Everstone's transfer." Looking towards the door, then turning back towards the family, she continued, "As part of the arrangements, The School shall waive all dues – both monetarily and of service – while Miss Everstone is among our advanced curriculum. Should she wish to stay within the dormitories at any later time, I shall override any collection as well." Focusing only on Cora, she concluded while placing her arm on the student's shoulder, "Your sole charge is to blossom into the lovely flower your mother and father know you will become."

While the Head Instructor gave her farewell, the family embraced one another. As they displayed their unity, Aeyra said to the departing elf, "Our Cora, our little tulip, will make you proud."

Continuing with her exit, the Arch Magister did not stop, but replied before crossing the door's threshold, "I know she will."

CHAPTER EIGHT:

"THE KIND AND THE COLD"

After a much needed respite from the recent nightmare, Cora entered The School's hall the next morning with an energetic wave directed at her mother and father that had just dropped her off at the threshold. As her parents departed, she initiated her pace down the hall she had grown accustomed to.

She was anxious but excited, eager for what seemed to be yet another first day, despite her having had a recent orientation just a few weeks ago. While the thought caused her nerves to slightly elevate, she was distracted as she began to hear familiar voices that warmed her heart from her old classroom on her left hand side.

Noticing their former pupil who walked through the hall, some of the children began to shout aloud.

"Cora!"

"We have some new treats to share!"

"See you at the banquet hall for lunch," they said.

As she started to wave and even share some words through her wide smile, Instructor Pepperton calmly hushed the class, then made his way outward. Crossing into the hall, he said with a cheerful smile, "Miss Everstone, it truly has been a pleasure to be your Instructor these last few weeks." While Cora grew delighted with the comments, he continued, "We look forward to watching you grow here within The School. Yet, you should not linger. You would not want to arrive tardy to your new class, would you?"

Agreeing with the former Instructor, Cora shook her head, then lunged towards his waist and gave him a warm embrace. Gently hugging the child back, he said, "We will miss you, too." Withdrawing from the hold, he finished, "Now show your new class what a wonderful student you are."

Happily, Cora agreed and made her way down the corridor after parting from her former peers. With each step, she recalled to herself the instructions she was given in reaching her new class. First, she took a right, then a left, and lastly moved down a longer hall that held an elegant archway. Having arrived at the partition where the High Elf classes began, she pushed open the first door on her right as she had been advised to do.

Instead of hearing the typical noise of talking children that she had grown accustomed to when entering, all she heard was the lightly creaking hinges of the carved door as it moved inward to a silent room. Since she looked down after having put all of her weight into the heavy door, she began to worry that perhaps she had arrived at an incorrect destination.

After a brief pant, she tilted her head upwards and was slightly startled. To her surprise, the room was full – though with only half the number of students as her former group.

Unlike Pepperton, the Instructor of this class did not acknowledge her, so Cora tried to greet her new teacher.

"Good morning," she said politely towards the male elf. "I'm Cora Everstone."

Rather than return the introduction, the elven teacher only sat in his chair. After finishing one last inscription onto a parchment atop his engraved desk, he dropped his quill, then pointed towards the right rear of the room with his head still down. Retracting his hand almost immediately with a rigid motion, the Instructor did not share any other action or even a word as he reassumed his writing.

Shying away from the rude interaction, Cora bashfully tucked her head in, then made her way down the furthest aisle on her right. As she crossed the first seat, she lifted herself a bit and initiated a smile to the first pair of students, but they paid her no mind. Despite being unwelcomed, she continued her polite manners and extended her silent, cheerful expression to those around, but the older students simply stared forward or away from her.

With none returning any courtesy towards her, Cora adjusted her focus to her newly assigned seat. Yet, she noticed it was vastly different from the rest. The others had stained designs and were coated in gloss; while hers was dull, worn, and isolated – hidden in the back as the only desk in the rear row.

In just the few short moments within her new class, she could feel the difference between Pepperton's atmosphere and this one that felt rigid, even uninviting.

Quiet and now feeling a somber attitude brewing within her, Cora decided to just take her seat after setting her pack down. As no books or supplies awaited her, she began to unload her old quill and the worn parchment paper she carried with her. Prompted by her actions, a pair of students from the middle and far left aisle in the row just in front peered at her.

Visibly, the male and female pair held back a chuckle that was aimed towards mocking their new classmate.

Feeling ashamed, Cora put her head down and tried to pay them no mind. She kept low and forward, only staring at the tips of the long, dark brown hair from the other female elf that sat in front of her.

As an awkward minute passed, the Instructor's chair could be heard pressing backwards against the floor – startling Cora and causing her to gaze upward. She watched as the teacher initiated a light cough to clear his throat, then started his early morning speech, but only to be halted as the door to his left pushed open.

Entering with a commanding stride, the cherry and white-haired Arch Magister popped in and went directly towards the Instructor. After a brief stare aimed at the rear of the class, she said, "Limrich, a word. Now." In an irritated manner, the Head Instructor of The School could be seen visibly lecturing her subordinate, but in a low enough whisper that none around could hear.

Attempting to clarify between the Head Instructor's words, the teacher explained, "She came from twenty-five, we were twelve, and have made room for thirteen – an odd figure."

As the Arch Magister pressed him further, the male Instructor continued, "And she shall receive them. They shall be distributed after her introduction to us all, just as the human classes have done before."

After a last set of words directed at him, the Arch Magister pulled back, causing the male Instructor to add, "I concur, our goal is to welcome her as one of our own."

"Very well," responded the Head Instructor. With a nod, she concluded in a loud voice for those around, "You may proceed, Instructor Ravenbeak."

While the Arch Magister made her exit, the elven Instructor called towards his newest student. "Miss Everstone," he said. "Come forward."

Just as she had done before in Pepperton's classroom, Cora took a step up and made her way to the head of the class. Her thoughts shifted towards hope as she paced on, feeling as if the recent negativity she felt towards her would be lifted after an introduction to her new peers and soon-to-be friends.

"Present yourself," said the Instructor in a tone that hinted of mild frustration, "then receive your supplies." As he withdrew a set of books and writing materials from his cabinet, he pounded them onto his desk while adding, "Keep it brief so as not to upset the lesson plan."

"Hello," she started with a shy smile towards the cold stares peering at her. Feeling somewhat timid among the students who looked like young adults, she crossed her slightly sweaty palms behind her, then continued, "I'm Cora Everstone. This is my first year at The School and I'm excited to…"

Interrupted by several hands that were raised, the Instructor halted Cora's speech as he called forth one of the other students. Maintaining her seat, the female elf asked towards Ravenbeak, "Instructor, do the Arulonians not have their own academy? Why would a peasant girl of theirs be among our class?"

"Excellent question," responded the Instructor in an arrogant tone that was dismissive of Cora.

Before the teacher finished his thought, another student with his hand raised shouted out of turn, "Is she from the south, or perhaps a Dwarf of the north? She is quite, small."

"A Lesser Elf has more weight," interrupted another pupil. "She is underfed."

"All proper inquiries for our 'gifted' student," encouraged the Instructor. "Yet, it seems she comes to us from Riverbend – a family of gardeners as I have been informed." Turning towards the human child, he said, "Now if you will, return to your seat so we may resume our lessons. This introduction is concluded." While walking over to the large parchment board, he finished, "And do not forget your books."

With tears forming in her eyes and a bright red glow setting itself atop her cheeks, Cora did as she was told. Using all of her might, she lifted the larger texts and materials provided to her. Moving slowly at first, she only picked up her pace when her thoughts shifted to reaching her seat and putting her head down.

Yet, she struggled. The books were too heavy for her and the dangling supplies were not easy to uphold. Reaching the second-to-last row, she dropped the bottom text along with a tear that splattered itself against the clean tile.

Rather than help, the student that sat in front of her just stared forward in silence while the male from behind whispered, "Is the green-thumb Dwarf not strong enough?"

"Seems so, Deverin," answered the female in the far left row. "Her grip is as poor as her rags."

Embarrassed and ridiculed, Cora began to lose hold of the next book. She tumbled and shook forward – rattling the book from her hands, but did not hear a sound of it falling.

Instead, the book was suspended in the air – being held by the female High Elf that sat in front of Cora who caught it only to preserve her elbow from being struck. Without looking at the human girl, she turned and placed the book on the desk behind her, then resumed her stare forward with her deep, green eyes.

"T-Thank you," stuttered Cora as she was relieved to have been helped.

Despite the kindness she tried to offer, Cora received no reply, rather she only heard the booming voice of the Instructor as he said, "Your seat, now."

In a hustled movement, Cora quickly placed the remaining supplies on her desk, then reached towards the fallen book. While she bent down in a flustered manner, the two elves to her sides continued their banter as they further chuckled and berated her in a low voice.

"Varissa, look. This stray Dwarf is faster than we thought," commented Deverin.

"A trait certainly not acquired from her brown-bottom parents who sit on the ground all day," replied the female after a giggle.

Visibly growing exhausted of the remarks as the human girl returned to her seat, the female elf in front of Cora twisted her head towards the two at her right – flinging her pony-tail and the two braids of hair that hung at each side. "Quiet already," she lashed out.

First, the two checked on the Instructor who carried on with the start of the lesson, then they looked to Cora as she had most of her face huddled between her arms. Turning their attention to the elf who attempted to pacify them, they began to mock her instead.

"The old one finally speaks," said Deverin.

"Perhaps being held back from The School was not her only delay," jested Varissa.

Since they could not get a rise out of the female elf who only kept gazing forward to the Instructor, the two elves slowed themselves for a moment, but diverted to Cora when she raised her head to speak.

With a set of tears falling down each eye and a puffed, red face, Cora begged, "Please, stop."

Although her comment was aimed solely at the pair of scornful High Elves, she caught the attention of the Instructor that scolded aloud, "Miss Everstone, if you would be so kind as to stop interrupting."

As the teacher resumed his lecture, Cora felt ashamed and further saddened. Her mind wanted to stay attentive to the discussion, but her spirit had been battered too much in such a short time. Seeking to shy away from those nearby that belittled her, Cora slid her face back into her arms that rested atop the desk but kept both ears uncovered – allowing her to listen in as the Instructor spoke about their upcoming magical assessment that very afternoon.

CHAPTER NINE:

"AFTERNOON SURPRISE"

As the morning lessons about introductory spells and its language went on, Cora's mood shifted from feeling melancholic to focused. With the students busy attending to the Instructor's lecture, she was able to concentrate and recall the positive encouragement her parents and the Arch Magister had just given her – driving her to jot down notes faster than any other in class atop the fresh parchment she was given.

Yet in spite of her speed, it seemed to not be enough as some of the material was incomplete and even unknown to her – all seemingly part of some advanced coursework that she had never covered before the transfer. The language was difficult for her to understand and even more challenging to write as it was a dialect she had never spoken before, of strange sounds and syllables that Instructor Pepperton seldom used.

Still, she pressed on, not letting the unfamiliar material get the best of her. While she wrote, she even peered towards the large texts – scrambling through its pages to find the references said by Instructor Ravenbeak. In her attempt to compensate for the lessons missed, she filled up multiple pages of scribbled notes and covered several borders of her books with scrawled page marks and comments – all in a few short hours.

Without pause in her work, she kept on until the Instructor called for a recess by directing all of his students to rise. While making a mention of the lunch being served at The School's banquet hall, he managed to rile up Cora's appetite and cause her stomach to growl.

Worried about any sounds she was making that could be the cause of further humiliation, Cora moved her idle hand to her belly, but soon felt relieved as any noise emanating from her was drowned out by the Instructor's continued commands.

"One orderly file," he said. "Nice and neat, standing tall."

Being much shorter than the High Elves that reached even upwards of six feet in length, Cora received a scoffed remark from Deverin and Varissa that stood just in front of her. While they bantered her, she tucked her head in low, but was called out once more.

"Tall I said, Miss Everstone," shouted the Instructor.

Having received such unwanted attention, Cora pulled her head high, but did so with a blushed face and glossy eyes that fought hard to hold back any weeping.

"Very good," commented the Instructor as he observed his line of students. With another command, he ordered the pupils to begin their march outward and into the hall.

In a single line, Cora trot behind the older female elf that sat in front of her – watching as her dark brown hair swayed from left to right. Carrying the mostly full bag of taffy in her left hand near her pocket, Cora could only think of wanting to share one with her. She had kept count of the remaining pieces and knew she had just enough to give to her former peers in Pepperton's class and to the elf who caught her falling book. As she thought out the idea of making a new friend, she let out a subtle smile while quietly pacing at the end of her line.

As she kept thinking of ways to gain favor and befriend the rest, Cora's ideas were interrupted as the Instructor boomed his voice once more.

"To our seats," he said.

Noticing they had already crossed into the banquet hall, Cora delighted in its familiarity. From the carved tables to the fine adornments, all was as she remembered, but from a different angle as she approached a new seating arrangement.

As they passed by the human classes towards a rear set of tables, the other elves in her group paid no attention to them, but Cora could not help but wave and smile towards many that she had already acquainted herself with. Cheerfully, some returned the gestures and smiles towards the kind Everstone child, but Instructor Ravenbeak became alerted to it.

Pacing around, he moved between them all and let off a stern expression – requesting Pepperton's class face back towards themselves.

"To our current seats," reminded the bothered Instructor towards his newest student. "Not former ones."

Once more, Cora's smile was turned to a frown since the High Elves clearly treated her differently than the rest. As her facial expression changed, so did her mood as it went from being lifted in seeing her companions towards feeling ashamed. Now being ushered to her seat, Cora sat right next to the older elf with her back away from Pepperton's class and across from Deverin and Varissa, who did not hesitate to mock her pouted expression with their pretentious mannerisms.

"Who would have thought they could turn so red," said Deverin with a pompous smirk.

Directing her attention to both Cora and the elf that was visibly a decade older than the rest, Varissa added, "At least she can dry her eyes onto the sleeve of the mute."

Although no reaction was gained by insulting the oldest student, the youngest did the opposite. As the tears she held back started rolling down her eyes, Cora tilted her head downward – tucking it between the table and her chest. She tried to control her sobbing, but she was unable to. Yet, it did help as her own sound muffled all the rest, particularly the two bantering High Elves.

While Cora desired to keep hidden from everyone, she was forced to peek her head up when several loud thuds rang atop the table she ducked under. Being placed in front of her as she rose were several large dishes of toasted almonds, honey wheat loaves, and freshly picked berries; along with several glasses of a lightly gold juice and fresh water.

Ignoring the rest of the platters that were being laid down consisting of cooked fowl and steamed greens, Cora went right for the juice and a slice of bread. First, she sipped on the sweet-tasting beverage of white grapes and honey, then cut a piece of the freshly baked bread with her utensils. Despite her attempts to act politely and with proper manners, it still caught the attention of the two relentless elves that mocked her for using cutlery on sliced bread.

Seeking a way out from those who stared at her while she ate, Cora simply grabbed the remaining slab of the honey wheat toast that was on her plate and brought it to her chest.

Lowering her head again, she kept it tucked and away from the High Elves that continued to pester her.

As time went on during their noon lunch, the two elves began to shift their attention from Cora and diverted it to the food they ate while conversing with the rest around them. Feeling a tad safer, Cora peeked her head out and picked up the napkin on her dining set, then wiped her mouth. While she laid the cloth piece down, she became startled by the precise hands of an attendant that removed it along with several plates and silverware from those who had finished their meals.

Knowing that dessert would take another few minutes to arrive, Cora took the time to reach into the bag of taffy and pull one out for her neighbor.

"My Momma and Poppa," she said towards the older elf, "they took me to the market for some treats. Would you like one?"

Turning to face her, the eldest student only looked, but did not respond as Cora continued, "It's honey-flavored taffy, from Hawlon Honeydew."

Nervous at the lack of reaction from her peer, she did not know what to do at first. But as the awkward second went by, Cora instinctively grabbed a drop of the dried candy, then placed it gently into the elf's palm that was nearest her.

Still, the High Elf did not move. She only stared at the piece of taffy and asked, "Why?"

Cora was shocked, but somewhat relieved that she was able to at least garner a response. Being the hopeful and kind girl that she was, she did her best to set aside the momentary anxiety and asked in a mild stutter, "I-I'd like to be your friend."

She waited for her remark to be reciprocated, but it seemed Cora was only able to withdraw the one word from the elf who silently clutched the piece of taffy. Feeling her time was short to distribute the rest, she did not linger and instead stood from her seat with the candy bag held in both hands.

Twisting towards Pepperton's class that was behind her, she began to move but was stopped by the loud yell of the Instructor who seemed to monitor her every move.

"Miss Everstone," he said while pacing rapidly towards her. "Where do you think you are off to?"

"I-I, umm," she stumbled. "I was going to share some treats with my friends."

Stripping the bag of waxed parchment from her, the Instructor furthered, "Goods from the market, it appears. Are the delicacies we provide not adequate enough for your tastes?" Without allowing the child to respond, he spun back to his position in the banquet hall and finished, "I shall be confiscating these. Back to your seat."

Cora's head was low, her face once more blushed, and her timid nature worsened as she returned to the two High Elves jesting about her acting as a mischief-maker. While returning to where she sat, she also noticed the taffy from the older elf's hand was gone. Since her would-be friend did not chew, Cora assumed the only piece of candy she had shared was simply thrown away.

The remaining lunch time felt slow and grueling for Cora as she could not help but sob at all of the hostility being aimed at her. For reasons she could not understand, the High Elves were relentlessly mean and dismissive of her. The more she pondered on the matter of her first day being transferred, the more she just wanted the afternoon to end so she could go home.

The desserts passed without Cora touching a single one. Sitting in a silent, somber mood, she only moved when the

Instructor called the class to exit after the human groups went before them.

"Single file back," he said aloud. "Should you require use of the facilities, do so before the assessment."

Some students initiated a stressed whisper as they discussed the upcoming examination, but Cora just kept to herself – worried that if she asked any questions towards any peer it may be misinterpreted.

While most of the class continued on and went towards their respective lavatory, Cora walked back towards the room with just a handful of others. In an attempt to avoid further ridicule, she sat back at her desk and kept her focus to the open books and scattered notes across her desk.

Although Cora desired to keep to herself, her attention was shifted to the sound of a familiar voice that entered the classroom.

"Instructor Ravenbeak," said the presumptuous Davik as he made his introduction into the room known. Acting as if he had seen an old friend, he continued in a loud, boastful manner, "Tell me, how are our two special students?"

"Grand Magister, my lord," bowed the Instructor. "They are proving to be quite… unique. Interesting, I would say."

"Very well," commented the Grand Magister as he stared only at the older elf that sat in front of Cora. "Do ensure they are given the utmost courtesy while they are in training. I expect the best for those who are to come under my service."

"I would dare provide no less for the head of our order," graciously responded Instructor Ravenbeak.

Following a bow that was exchanged among the two, the Grand Magister parted while the Instructor continued readying several papers for the upcoming assessment.

Curious about their interaction, Cora asked towards the elf in front of her, "Did you transfer, too?"

For a second, Cora waited for a reply that was not given. Reaching out her hand, she moved her index finger to tap her peer's shoulder, but stopped when she felt a series of exhales coming from in front of her – ones that appeared to be full of agitation. Retracting her arm, Cora wanted to ask another question about the upcoming examination, but chose to keep quiet so as to not bother the elder elf and to avoid the two pestering classmates that were just returning to their seats.

"Seems the master has come to check on his pet," teased Deverin towards the older elf.

"Pets," corrected Varissa, who let out a brief giggle before taking to her chair.

Sitting quietly, Cora huddled inward in her discouraged state – only noticing the breathing of the student in front of her gain momentum after every word that was uttered from Deverin and Varissa. But still, the older elf did not return a remark.

With the last student trickling into the class, Instructor Ravenbeak shut the door to his room and called for silence. Stepping back to his desk, he gathered several handfuls of parchment and began passing them out to all of the students in the left aisle first, then the center, and lastly the right side where Cora sat.

Anxious and nervous, but excited to prove her studies over the last month, Cora was thrilled to receive the paper.

"Cora Everstone," she mumbled softly and to herself as she wrote down her name.

"Thirty-second day of fall," she continued as she marked the date. "Second Golden Era, Year Nine Hund-red and…"

Before finishing the last of the paper's heading, the Instructor echoed his voice around the class and caught the attention of all, "You have until the conclusion of this afternoon to turn in your assessment. There shall be no interruptions or intermissions, and no talking."

Acknowledging the instructions, Cora kept on with the front page, then flipped the tied booklet to the second. Seeing several lines that were open for writing, she grew elated as she was eager to elaborate on the history and lessons provided by Instructor Pepperton.

Despite her initial excitement, she started to grow confused at what she saw. Cora read the first of the examination's inquiries, but recalled none of the material – not even from the morning's lecture. Soon, she grew a sweat and began to take short, rapid breaths after realizing that each question on the first page was about the odd language she had never encountered before. Flipping through each other sheet, her panic only worsened when she concluded that the entire assessment was about a course she had never covered.

Setting down her writing instrument, Cora began to feel the rush of emotions as she put both hands to her face to hide the tears she felt would resume.

Not allowing even a moment to pass in her reaction, the Instructor walked up to Cora and said, "Is there an issue, Miss Everstone?"

Cora raised her head and saw the Instructor peering over her while all of the other students stopped their writing. As she wiped a droplet that fell down her cheek, the harsh teacher furthered, "Well?"

"I-Instructor," said Cora with a choked voice. "It's just, I wasn't…"

"You were not prepared for this assessment?" interrupted Instructor Ravenbeak. Continuing to jab at the weeping child, he went on, "You did not cover this material as you were too busy learning what we High Elves learn as children? Perhaps you are better off in the remedial lessons offered to your kind."

"N-no, I just," Cora cried. "I-I'll be prepared for the next, I want to stay, I…"

Furthering his dismissive nature towards her, the Instructor said, "Then, it is settled." Taking away her test, he continued, "You have failed this assessment." Walking away with the packet, he finished, "I shall look forward to the next."

As he walked back to his desk, the female elf in front of Cora slammed her fist onto her own exam after closing it shut. "So you can fail her again, then again for the Grand Magister?" she said aloud. "Quite fair of you, 'Instructor'."

Crumbling the paper in his hands, the upset teacher turned towards the shouting student and said, "What did you say, Miss Starborne?"

Looking firmly back at him, the older student replied, "I believe I did not stumble over my words, Instructor. Are you hard of hearing and perhaps in need of repeating?"

"Silence!" remarked Ravenbeak in frustration as he rushed over to her desk. Picking up the student's assessment packet in anger, he furthered, "You may join Miss Everstone in finding a seat at the banquet hall. Perhaps you can both come prepared to your next examination together."

Miss Starborne stood amid the chuckling of Varissa and Deverin as both sat behind the Instructor's slender frame. First, she stared up at the teacher that was nearly a half-a-foot taller than her, then she looked down to Cora.

"Come," said Miss Starborne.

Acknowledging her peer, Cora stood up after wiping away a set of teardrops. Without uttering another word towards the Instructor, both made their exit from the classroom and went on to the banquet hall as they were told.

While pacing a few steps behind, Cora tried to catch up to the larger strides taken by the elf that was almost as tall as her father. Attempting to gain her attention and slow her a tad, she asked, "Where do we go?"

Although she did not respond, Miss Starborne did slow to allow Cora to be at her side. When they went far enough into the hall and reached the dining area, she pointed towards the empty room and said, "Any seat."

Proceeding to the first group of tables where the human classes usually sat, Cora set herself while the elf followed.

Staring at her fellow student, Cora wiped a drying drop off her cheek, and said, "T-Thank you." While the older student stared off to her surroundings, she continued, "I thought you didn't like me."

Still not offering another word, Miss Starborne only reached into her pocket after looking back to Cora. From her more elegant attire, she pulled out a small, bundled napkin, then displayed the piece of honey taffy given to her – perfectly intact.

Extending the candy outward, the elf asked, "Half?"

"No," said Cora politely and in a kind tone. "I shared it with you, it's yours."

Despite her face being firm, the elven student could not hide the short, subtle smile that grew on her face. Turning back to her usual stern stare, she said, "Half, then."

Grabbing the taffy at the middle, Miss Starborne tugged at the elastic treat until it gave. Successfully splitting it in two, she threw one morsel in her mouth, then handed her new friend the other.

Reluctantly but happily, Cora accepted the taffy she had enjoyed before. In unison, both began to chomp on the chewy candy as vigorously as one another while enjoying its taste. While both sat and relished in each other's company, the elven student only offered one more word as a way of introducing herself, though informally.

"Tamyn," she said.

CHAPTER TEN:

"ATTUNED"

J oining class the following morning as early as she could, Cora sought to obtain a head start in the course material for that day. Or at least she had told her parents.

Secretly, she wanted to get there before any other so she would not have to endure the stares offered by the rude students and the harsh Instructor as she made her way down the aisle. If she had her head buried in the texts, she felt the rest of the world around her would fade.

It was an effort that, as time moved on in the early hours, appeared to prove correct as none around her seemed to bother. Moving onto past chapters and lessons she had missed, Cora was able to go over some of the initial syllables and words of the old, broken language she was trying to learn.

As the minutes flew by, Cora began to mumble to herself as she attempted to make out the odd words that made little sense the more she read.

"Sum, some, so mad," she whispered to herself with a struggled speech.

While trying different pronunciations of the isolated word that was part of an incomplete sentence, Cora heard a bump and a thud from the desk in front of her, then the voice of her new friend as she took her seat.

"So-may-eh," corrected Tamyn. "Somaedh."

Peeking her head upwards and away from the pages she was buried in, Cora saw the calm and somewhat stern face of Tamyn. Following the example she was given, she attempted to recite the pronunciation once. Since her elven friend did not react, Cora tried again, then received a nod before Tamyn returned to gaze forward.

Proud that she got her first word correct, Cora smiled and said towards Miss Starborne, "Thank you." Realizing the class was filling up with other students that remained mostly quiet, she continued in a softer tone, "And good morning."

Without turning around or moving her head, Tamyn whispered back, "To you as well."

Hearing the returned greeting, Cora kept up her cheerful grin, then bobbed her head downward as she sought to return to her books. Yet, she was caught off her guard as the pompous voice of Deverin pierced her concentration in the middle of her motion.

"Quite the luck we seem to have," he said sarcastically as he referenced the spell's name. "If she had a wand with her, we would all certainly be asleep by now."

Chuckling from the seat behind, Varissa continued in a low tone, "Seems we have some more entertainment to look forward to from our favorite, dysfunctional pair."

In a calm and collected manner, Tamyn did her best to yet again not let her emotions show. Instead of verbally responding to their bantering, she turned towards the two other High Elves and stared at them with her usual, firm look.

Sensing the intimidation from his peer, Deverin returned to facing forward as did Varissa, but not before he mumbled, "In a foul mood, it seems."

Cowardly looking away, Varissa added, "Just as she was yesterday with the Instructor. Quite good it did for her on the assessment."

Being the closest to her, Deverin did his best to conceal his words as Tamyn balled up her right fist. But the egotistical, unrelenting student could not help but make a brief, additional comment, "I wonder how they fared on it."

While Varissa let out a slight giggle, Deverin stayed quiet as Tamyn began to clench her other fist and bring them together. As her facial expression grew clearly agitated, she was halted when the Instructor closed the classroom doors and made his announcements.

"Class," said the Instructor. Without need to say any other word, all of the students settled down and looked forward at him, causing him to continue, "Although two of our disruptive students failed their assessments yesterday afternoon, it appears we shall be continuing with our lesson plan for all, or so I have been informed. This morning, we will press on without recess once again as all shall be dismissed around noon in honor of the jubilee and its celebration this coming afternoon and evening."

Being the first grand holiday she would experience with her parents within the capital city, Cora became thrilled. Her excitement grew so much that she started to muffle out the rest of the words said by the mean Instructor as she focused on the cheerful event her family and those close to her would delight in.

Concluding his statements, Cora only resumed her attention towards the Instructor when he called for one of the larger texts to be opened, while asking to place any others in the basket below their desk. Following his commands, she did as she was told – turning to the first page and readying herself for the coming lesson.

"Enchanted gems," said Instructor Ravenbeak as he went towards his board. While drawing out several designs and shapes of crystals, he continued, "They are the catalyst which attunes our magic and allows us to channel them properly into the spells we so desire. Their abilities to focus, even harness the power within us, is what makes them so valuable to our order." Moving on to elaborate on some more of his designs, he went on, "We rely on them just as much as a Highguard does their blade, for without them, the resulting magic would be wild and clumsy if even summoned at all." Now underlining his markings, he turned around towards the class and finished, "Yet, they are not infallible and in need of us as much as we are in their need. They are a tool, one used solely by those familiar with them and by those who have the power to channel spells through them. Should the skill and knowledge not match that which you intend to incant, then the results could be devastating to it and its bearer."

While putting down the chalk and pacing towards the classroom door, Instructor Ravenbeak resumed, "In this classroom, we shall exercise the utmost caution with only initiate spells that are not as severe or taxing towards our magisters in training." Holding the door's handle, he said, "As your skills improve and as your lessons advance, more shall be required of you. Yet for this morning, you need only worry about choosing the right gem for you, or being chosen by it if you are one of the few fortunate enough."

Pulling the wooden door frame back, the Instructor revealed a fellow High Elf that was waiting across the hall. Being signaled inward, the assistant rolled in a moving table with several covered displays.

"As we only specialize in one form of the five various schools of magic," said the Instructor, "you each shall be given an opportunity to select from the gem that corresponds with your predisposition." As the moving table was laid to rest in the center of the room, Instructor Ravenbeak stared over to Cora and continued, "That is, if you are even aware of what your calling is." Gazing around to the rest of the room, he finished, "Although, I do not foresee this being a concern for the vast majority of you as earlier schooling and placement should have already shown such a result."

With the assistant's help, the Instructor lifted up the elegant silk cloth that covered the display – revealing a tiered set of shimmering stones and crystals that were colored in various shades of yellow, white, red, blue, and green. Caught by its allure, Cora was the only to display her fascination vocally as the rest of her peers remained silent.

Uninterrupted by his youngest student's brief vocalization and the attendant who cleaned off any wandering articles of dust, Instructor Ravenbeak moved to the forward area of the arrangement's carved frame. After settling at its center, he then called out, "Mister Spearhawk, come forward, if you please."

As the young, but developed High Elf stood up, he took a deep breath. Initiating his pace forward, he did so in a prideful stride – acting as if this moment was what would mature him from adolescence to adulthood. With grace, he drew his hand close towards the gold and amber colored gems, then selected a dazzling citrine.

Prompted by this honorable moment, the Instructor said, "An Invoker as our first, always a pleasant sign from Deol himself."

Calling forth the next pupil, Instructor Ravenbeak went on down the line from the left aisle first. Anxiously, Cora awaited in her seat – attempting to hide her emotions and excitement until she was asked to rise. With each gem that was plucked out, she grew further unsettled, soon even concerning herself about the various colors and if she would know which one to pick. Her restlessness only further propounded when she saw the entire left aisle went, then the center along with most of the right.

As the only other remaining student in front of her, Tamyn was ordered to come forward by the Instructor, but in a more apprehensive manner than the rest received. In a proud motion like the others had done, she ignored the unkind eyes and even gestures – making her way up the class.

Unlike the rest of those before her, Miss Starborne stood out in front of the batch of gems that were white in color. Extending her hand outward but above the display, she closed her eyes and waited.

Prompted by her action, the Instructor said, "This is not a…"

Frozen by the sound of a gentle breeze emanating from the stones, Instructor Ravenbeak was interrupted. While Tamyn kept her reach extended, a small, quartz crystal swirled with a tiny burst of air that only slightly separated itself from the others. After being the only one to magically remove it from the set, Tamyn gently bowed her head in defiance of the Instructor, then returned to her seat after nodding towards Cora.

As the last and the youngest to have her attempt, Cora became so nervous that she first stumbled out from her seat –

striking her elbow onto her desk. Before any chuckles could erupt, Tamyn hushed loudly towards her peers, then waved her hand forward for her friend to move down the aisle.

Without any other sound or obstacle, Cora pressed on to the front of the class and stood before what she felt was another test. Standing just tall enough to reach the display, she peered first at all of the blue colored pieces, then took a step back.

Turning to her Instructor as she was unsure of which to grab, she nervously asked in an attempt to delay her interaction, "T-The gem, where do we keep it? I don't have a necklace or locket."

Shaking his head, the Instructor replied, "These are not simple gems meant for common jewelry. These shall be in your possession until they are placed into a wand or weapon, yet that is for another lesson." Ushering her back towards the arrangement of stones, he said, "We do not have all morning, Miss Everstone."

Taking a gulp and a heavy breath, Cora took her step forward and got right up to the display of blue gems again. From azures to zircons and sapphires, she tried to absorb it all within the few seconds she felt she was allotted. The decision was seemingly difficult for her as she was additionally not one for trinkets and finery, coming from her simplistic lifestyle. Yet, the choice seemed to make itself as she heard a light gush coming from the centermost aquamarine.

Now visible to the entire class, the soft flow turned into a tiny spout that lifted the gem upwards and towards Cora. Previously shocked at the sight of Tamyn's process, the class grew completely silent in their astonishment as now a human child was being called by a gem. Cora, too, even felt the same wonder and amazement as she briefly stayed frozen – stuck staring at it.

Rattling off the momentary feeling, Cora took another deep inhale, then a relieving exhale. Extending her forearm outward, the excitement building up in her caused flutters to form in her stomach, but she was able to set them aside as she opened her palm towards the gem.

As the aquamarine began to settle into her hands, she felt its weight grow exponentially heavy. While the water spout flashed upwards and into several long strings, Cora was shoved downward and into the classroom floor.

Holding the gem tightly in her right hand, Cora started to push herself up with her left arm, but felt the floor as soft and mushed with blades of grass encircling her fingers – causing her to stop. Startled and even dazed by the fall, she started to wonder if a spell was cast to prevent her from hurling herself onto the hard tile.

However, it all seemed to be wrong and out of place. After the brief muffling of her ears wore away, she started to hear what sounded as a nearby flow of water and when she began to blink her eyes, all she saw was a cloudy sky with the sun cutting through its bundled formations. Looking around while she stood up, she started to realize it was a familiar setting – one she desired not to return to.

Before her panicked breath could kick in, all she heard was the recognizable voice of the High General as he shouted aloud, "Shields!"

Turning to face the crest of the hill, Cora saw the five elves alongside their commander. As they all huddled closely, she stared up to see what it was they were protecting themselves from.

Lingering in the sky, Cora saw a hail of arrows that darkened the day as they rained down upon the stream's location.

Instinctively, she closed her eyes and screamed out loud in fear to counter the sounds of the diving arrows and the rushing enemy that trampled on behind them.

Not feeling any pain or hearing any other noise, Cora only laid still until she was called by a calm, although unpleasant voice.

"Miss Everstone," said the unenthused Instructor. "If you would kindly return to your seat after your little display, it would be very much appreciated."

"M-my, my what?" Cora stuttered. "How, where am…"

"Your seat, now," interjected Ravenbeak.

Moving down to physically lift her up, the Instructor propped Cora upright and pointed her down the right aisle.

Shaken from the brief vision, Cora took a few seconds before her first step, but started her way down to her desk shortly while hearing the whispers of those around her.

"How did she do that?"

"Who is she?"

"Those pointed arrows from that spout."

"Just how?" they said.

Growing inattentive to the rumors and words being spoken about her, Cora only worried about her head that began to thump with a light pain. As she reached her seat, she laid the aquamarine onto the desk and cradled the back of her head while sitting down in visible pain.

While the sounds grew louder of those speaking about the intriguing event, Cora started to move her head downward as she still clutched it. She wanted the pain as well as the gossip to stop, but she did not have the courage to speak aloud.

Despite her desire, she did not have to make a sound as her friend in front of her spoke out, "Quiet!" Turning towards Cora while still in her seat, Tamyn asked, "How badly are you hurt?"

"I-It stings, my head," responded the ailing Cora with a stutter as she was embarrassed after what had just happened. Seeking no further attention, she said, "I'm fine, I think."

"You are not," said Tamyn as she rose to her feet. Lifting Cora up gently and grabbing her gem for her, she continued towards the Instructor, "I shall be taking her to the infirmary."

"With whose permission?" questioned the unconcerned teacher.

Pacing forward as if his words meant nothing to her, Tamyn responded while moving alongside Cora towards the front, "With the Arch Magister's, if I must."

Letting out a light huff, Instructor Ravenbeak gave no further argument towards the student's request. Although he did not aid Cora as he simply returned to his chair instead, the first student to grab his own stone, Mister Spearhawk, stood up to open the classroom door while he gave a respectful and concerned bow to the pair.

CHAPTER ELEVEN:

"THE SORROWFUL CELEBRATION"

S taring at the etched stone that ran horizontally along the nearby wall, Cora slowly counted its patterns and markings as she rested on her side. Laying atop a comfortable, feathery mattress, she did not have much to do besides occupy her time with the mundane and wonder what was being discussed in class. Despite her accelerated mind, she did as she was previously bid to do and tried to keep her body as still as possible while the bump and pain from the back of her head receded.

Growing hungrier with each passing second, Cora started to realize that the noon hour was approaching as well as the time for her early dismissal. All she could think of was getting up, heading home, and joining her parents along with a few school friends for a meal from the city market she had come to enjoy.

As her mind started to revolve around the thought of food and the upcoming celebration, she heard the infirmary's door opening from behind.

"Miss Everstone," said the approaching, warm female voice, "try not to move just yet, not until I check your bandage."

Coming up to her side and peeking over her hair, the restorative magister said, "Seems the spell and the medicine took hold quite well, the bump is healing nicely and is mostly gone."

With a smile and a kind expression of gratitude, Cora sat patiently as the rest of the dressing was unraveled from her head. Comforting her and providing some wisdom, the gentle woman said, "As much as I delight in a visit from such a kind student, please be sure to watch your step next time around."

Nodding her head, Cora acknowledged with a smile. As she rustled her hair to remove any knots formed by the bandage, she offered, "Thank you, Magister Arcona."

Helping the young student up to her feet, the thoughtful woman added, "You are quite welcome, Miss Everstone. Or before I know it, I will be saying Magister Everstone." Returning the cheerful grin given to her, Magister Arcona looked with pride towards the student and asked, "Do you know which individual schooling of magic you will be studying?"

"Well," thought Cora, "I've just gotten my blue gem."

Checking her pockets, Cora had a momentary panic as she could not find her recently received stone, prompting the older magister to remark, "Your friend has it, the student who brought you. Miss Starborne, I believe." Pointing towards the door, she went on, "She is waiting for you outside – arrived just a few moments ago." While Cora grew visibly eased, the soft-spoken healer carried on, "Blue means your gifts come from the waters of Azuricar and you will train as a Sorceress – a great one in the making, I can tell. Your first attunement stone is always a special one, some do not even let it go after training." Sharing a wink, she continued, "Do try to always keep it by your side." Directing Cora's body towards the exit, she finished, "Now that you are healed, run along with your friend. The festivities for the Jubilee of the Four Stars is set to begin shortly. You would not want to miss them."

Excitedly, Cora gave her farewell to the kind magister, then made her leave from the infirmary's quarters. Pulling the door, she saw Tamyn patiently sitting atop one of the few chairs in the waiting room. Before the elven student could stand up, Cora rushed her for a hug.

Embracing Tamyn's shoulder that stood near her eye level even while she sat, Cora exclaimed, "Thank you."

Although she did not react emotionally, Tamyn returned, "You are welcome." Lifting herself up and through Cora's hold, she continued, "We should go."

"We've been dismissed?" asked Cora. As her friend nodded, she inquired further, "Did I miss much in class?"

While tilting her head and stepping towards the hall, Tamyn said, "We can study after, the week's end approaches."

Catching the hint that her elven friend wanted to make her exit, Cora asked one last question, "So we may go to the festival now?"

Confirming with a nod, Miss Starborne let the inquisitive, youthful mind of Cora know that it was alright to exit – even without their class to ease her worries. Taking another set of paces, she began to lead the eager human child outward from The School's hallway and to the paved streets of the city's central section.

As they both reached the outside, they felt the warm, noon sun on their fair skin while their eyes glared from the light that was brighter than the passage they were in.

Hearing cheers and chants from all around, Tamyn said while motioning towards the populated celebratory areas by the palace, "This way."

"Wait," said Cora as she stopped just behind. "My Momma and Poppa, I have to go home."

Allowing Cora to lead on, Tamyn followed at her side. As they moved through the inner section and towards the northeastern one where Cora resided, both saw the extravagant displays that had been erected. Having clearly seen them before, Tamyn was not as fascinated as Cora who awed at it all – from the small stages where performers acted out, to the exciting festival games, and even every bit of special cuisine that was prepared in honor of the celebration.

Cora wanted to stop and absorb it all, but she kept on reminding herself that her family, and even some of her friends, were waiting on her back home. So she pressed on, walking alongside her High Elven companion through crowds and vendors, tents and shops. In a hurry, she tried to make it as fast as she could, but the vast number of citizens that were out made it more difficult for her.

Still, the pair arrived within the noon hour at the humble cottage. Politely, Tamyn hung back a few steps while Cora went up to the door and knocked once, then almost twice.

As if she was being waited on, the second thump of Cora's hand barely touched the oaken planks of the frame as it pulled inward.

"Cora," said her mother in a slightly alarmed voice. "We were starting to get worried when you didn't arrive with your friends." Pointing back towards the forward room and to the two children who patiently sat, she continued, "Emmie and Grayce are already here."

Although she was being pointed inside, Cora stood by the threshold as she introduced her new friend that stood idly behind her, "Momma, this is Tamyn."

Greeting her with a cheerful expression, the mother went forward and welcomed, "Please, Tamyn, come inside. We've heard all about you as well, from Cora's new class. I'm Aeyra, her mother." Looking down to Cora with a wink, she amended, "Her Momma." Ushering the still-standing elven student inside once more, she furthered, "Please, join us if you will. We'll be heading to the festival in just a moment."

Tamyn hesitated at first as she kept a firm, somewhat awkward stance, but eased herself when Cora requested, "Please?"

Nodding her head, Tamyn then proceeded inward while offering a brief greeting to the kind mother. Following Cora in what seemed to be an unfamiliar setting for her, she again stood still until the other children approached.

After a short introduction with Cora, the first, taller child enthusiastically said, "I am Emmie, you can be my first High Elf friend."

"A-and I am Grayce," stuttered the second one in a bashful, but polite manner. "N-nice to meet you."

As the three children exchanged a few words, Tamyn kept silent – observing the conversing trio that was visibly much younger than her.

Nudging Tamyn out of her quiet state, Emmie went on rapidly, "What is your favorite candy? I enjoy the pumpkin ones, any really. My mother always gets me some. Where is your family? Mine is joining us later, after work duties with father. Grayce's is back in Elarun, she stays in the dormitories, so hers are not coming."

Feeling slightly overwhelmed from the questioning and excited statements, Tamyn took a step back, but eased herself when Cora said, "Look, Tamyn." Pointing at the back of the hall, she said, "That's Poppa."

Closing the far bedroom door behind him, the content father peered outward to the new guest and said, "I'm Cehdric, Cora's father. Pleasure to meet you." Pacing in the hall towards his daughter, he went up to her and extended a layered jacket that he had just grabbed while saying, "In case it's too cold out tonight."

Happily agreeing, Cora threw the jacket over her dress, then smiled before embracing her father that knelt for her.

As he rose up, Cehdric peered slightly downward to his child's new friend that was a few inches shorter than he and said in a kind voice, "My apologies for keeping you." Gazing around to the rest in the room, he continued, "All of you, for waiting." Joining his wife's side, he clutched her shoulder and put his chin near the top of her head while asking, "Is everyone ready?"

With excitement and joy, the three children expressed their desires to join the festivities while the elf student simply nodded once. Clearly the most enthusiastic of them all, Emmie kept on spouting about different stalls and sights she wanted to visit while calling off delectable foods from each. Continuing on as they even crossed outward into streets, she did not stop until she heard Cora's stomach growl.

"Oh, you must be quite hungry," said Emmie while skipping her steps atop the stone. "Did you not have any snacks in class?" As Cora shook her head, she prodded further, "Why?"

"I, umm," stumbled Cora as she noticed her mother listening in on them from just behind, "I was in the infirmary."

Reacting as her daughter had expected, Aeyra stepped in and exclaimed, "What? Are you alright, honey? What happened?"

"I'm alright, Momma," said Cora in a shy, concealed manner. "I bumped my head is all."

"And how'd you do that?" asked the mother as she started examining her daughter and forcing everyone else to stop with her. "Where? I don't see it."

"Tamyn took me to the infirmary, Momma," answered Cora bashfully. "The nice lady magister there healed me after I fell."

While caressing her daughter, Aeyra turned to Tamyn and said, "Thank you, thank you so much." Sensing her daughter was withholding some of the details in her visibly embarrassed state in front of her friends, she begged, "But please, tell me how that happened."

Plucking a blue gemstone from her pocket and extending it outwards, Tamyn said, "She fell, holding this." After apologizing about her forgetfulness in giving it sooner, she handed it to Cora, who hesitated for a second to take it before shoving it immediately into her pocket.

"What's that?" asked Aeyra to the both of them.

Being the first to answer, Tamyn said, "An attunement crystal, for magic."

"Cora, honey," said the mother in a concerned voice, "did you see something? Is that why you fell down?"

As Cora's eyes welled up and a rosy color grew on her cheeks, she opened her mouth to talk, but was interrupted by her father.

"My love," he said as he clutched his wife gently to ease the tension and divert the subject, "you know she's as clumsy as..."

Stopping his own speech, Cehdric comically fumbled his feet to appear as if he was falling. As the children around him giggled, he recovered his balance and said, "As clumsy as me." Leaning down to Cora, he continued, "We can always speak later about our clumsiness. For now, let's get a bite to eat." Panning to the rest, he finished, "All of us."

His daughter and wife were the first to happily agree, followed by the animated Emmie who pointed at the nearby market. Hinting at her desire towards a stall close to them, she spoke about its warm, savory food and the sweet-tasting beverages offered.

As they all moved towards the delicious scent, they peeked at the intricate setup of iron pans atop a tempered flame next to a set of engraved tables lined with finely crafted silverware. After absorbing what the large booth had to offer, both parents pointed at the menu.

"Know what you'll be having, tulip?" asked Cehdric towards his daughter.

After catching its delectable, oily aroma, Cora aimed her finger at the scribbled description of the pan-fried, freshwater cod.

Witnessing the pointing child, the elven attendant at the stall said, "Comes with roasted fingerling potatoes. Is that fine?"

While Cora excitedly nodded, the booth's host went down the line – taking the orders of each and every person in the group, but halting when he reached Tamyn.

"My lady," he bowed towards her. Without another word as if he already knew what she desired, he went back to help his other fellows in preparing the dishes.

Prompted by the odd interaction, Emmie spouted off towards Tamyn, "How many times have you eaten here before? Their normal food is great, but the festival specialties are even better."

"First time," said Tamyn with a neutral tone compared to the child's excited voice.

As Emmie continued to pry, the elven attendant came back with several platters bundled in napkins atop twig-like frames and interrupted all manner of speech with just his presence. Having caught the attention of all with the mesmerizing aroma, he announced, "My lords and ladies, your order." Setting them down on a nearby table with the help of another, he continued, "One moment." Rushing back to grab a last tray full of mugs, he sped up, then returned. As he set a foamy, honey-scented beverage in front of each person, he said, "Our specialty. Juice for the little ones, ale for the adults. Do enjoy."

Initiating his walk away, Cehdric stopped the elven host and asked, "Wait, we haven't paid yet. How much?"

Turning around, the elven attendant once again bowed towards Tamyn and answered, "My lady and her friends do not pay here." Lifting himself up and cheerfully smiling while tilting his head, he finished, "Please, do enjoy."

Although Cehdric and Aeyra tried to stop the High Elf from leaving by taking out the few coins in their pockets, it did not help as he went off and away while ignoring them.

"Tamyn," said Aeyra, "please tell your friend we'll happily return the service if he has a garden he wishes us to tend. My husband and I both care for all manner of plants and flowers in the city, and also for anyone's home should they need."

"I can tell him," answered Tamyn. After a chug of her drink, she added in her usual neutral tone, "Yet, I do not know him or if he has a garden."

"You don't know him?" inquired Cehdric while raising his eyebrow.

"No," confirmed Tamyn who began to take heavy sips of her honey beverage to avoid conversation.

Sensing they were prying too much, Cora's parents halted any desire to ask any further questions and apologized while encouraging everyone to eat and delight in their meal.

Chomping on the crisped fish and mashing her teeth into the toasty potatoes, Cora began to visibly enjoy her late lunch just as much as Grayce and Emmie who delighted in their roast chicken. Within moments, all appetites were satisfied as even Emmie put down her plate to let out a light belch.

"Excuse me," she said with a smile – prompting those around her to chuckle, particularly her schoolmates.

Adding a few more jests and sparks of conversation, the group entertained one another until their parents reminded of the upcoming shows and tales. After cleaning the table and depositing their used utensils in a nearby bin, they all stood to make their way to the next spectacle.

In wonder and amazement, the three children went around leading as they stopped by each of the stands, acts, and displays – watching and admiring it all. With cheerful attitudes and awed smiles, they even caused Tamyn to forego her usual stern demeanor and take on a more joyful emotion.

Their day was becoming absolutely delightful, a sight the parents clearly relished in as they noticed all of Cora's worries and reservations seemingly fade away with each bit of laughter shared among her friends.

As the day grew late, the three girls started to wind their energy down and calm themselves. Looking to a nearby bench, Aeyra pointed as if she knew exactly where to stop for the day and said, "Let's take a bit of a rest, shall we?"

Agreeing as they were growing exhausted from all of the walking around, the children moved to the open seating. With several huffs and exhales, the trio sat – lifting up their feet in the process to relax and regain energy. Watching the display, Tamyn stood just by them with seemingly enough endurance left in her that she desired not to plant herself onto the bench as the others had done.

With Cehdric going off to purchase a few refreshments, Aeyra stayed to accompany the rest. Her head, though, was swiveling around as if looking for someone while she took care of the tired children. Right when she appeared to find what she was seeking, she waved.

"Over here!" she shouted.

Pacing through the massed crowd, a slightly rotund father and mother made their way towards her.

"So nice to see you all."

"We have finally arrived," they said.

Hearing the two, Emmie lifted her head and called out, "Mother, father!" As lively as ever, she rushed up to the two and embraced them.

As the Tenderlyn family held each other, the two parents offered their gratitude towards Aeyra, then asked where Cehdric was to thank him as well.

Returning just in time with four beverages huddled closely to his chest, Cehdric shared a few brief words while passing out the sweet-flavored drinks. "She's been wonderful," he said. "It was our pleasure."

"Yes," nodded Aeyra. "Thank you for letting her spend the day with Cora."

With a few more formalities and kind exchanges, the Tenderlyn family offered to take Grayce with them as her dormitories were on the way back towards their home. As the

Everstone parents agreed, the children and adults bid each other farewell and parted their ways.

Looking now back towards Cora and Tamyn with the setting sun facing her back, Aeyra said, "You're welcome to stay with us as long as you like."

"So long as our tulip can stay awake," jested Cehdric. "It's getting late for her."

Smiling back at her father, Cora returned towards him with a light yawn, "I'm still up, Poppa. Can we watch a bit of the night celebration?"

Happily, both of the parents agreed with a cheerful nod. Extending their hand outwards, they lifted Cora up. As she stood next to her elven friend, they readied themselves to walk closer to the upcoming display. First, Cehdric closed up her daughter's jacket for the colder temperatures the night would bring, then with a cheerful grin, he carried her up and propped her onto his chest with both arms.

"Is that better?" he asked.

"Yes, Poppa," smiled Cora as she could now see over the heads of the crowd and onto the stages that were being prepared throughout the sunset.

As the dusk settled, the once lively atmosphere shifted towards a more solemn tone – the crowds grew quiet, the merchants calmed themselves, and even the plays ceased their performances. Their surroundings became more silent as the last light faded and the night fully took hold.

Then, a wonderful display began – one that awed Cora instantly. Never before had she seen flying sparks and magical spells that lit up the sky in a wondrous fashion. Dazzled by the exhibition, she could not help but let out light gasps in her amazement – ones even shared by the two parents who also attended their first celebration in the High Elven capital.

The night sky was beautiful in her eyes, a sight Cora never wanted to end. Yet, it had to come to a conclusion to usher in the next portion of the ceremony.

Announcing just after the array of lights, several magisters boomed their voice to call for a moment of complete silence while everyone bowed their heads – an act to commemorate all those lost within the Age of Strife that lasted nearly a quarter century.

Although she and her parents did not have as much knowledge of its history as some of the High Elves around them that had clearly lived through it almost a millennium ago, the Everstone family gave their respects all the same. Being a courteous group, they did not begin to raise their heads until the moment passed and the others did so before them.

Being the first to caress his daughter, Cehdric said to her in a soft voice, "Truly beautiful isn't it, tulip?"

As she rest her head onto her father's shoulder, Cora nodded with a slightly deeper yawn.

While Aeyra and the rest of the family drew close to one another, a regal female voice came from behind, adding to Cehdric's sentiment, "Indeed it is."

Moving to face the person that spoke, Aeyra and Cehdric turned around to look at Tamyn who was flanked by an ageless female and male elf – both mid-sized for their race and of flawless complexion.

"I hear this is your first jubilee," said the female to the far right. "I am Amalyn Starborne, Tamyn's mother." As the taller male bowed his head alongside her, she continued, "On behalf of the Starborne family, we welcome you to the Golden Citadel." Before the two human parents could get a word out, Amalyn added, "We are friends of Astrael

Ashmane and have heard your child may be in need of a few additional lessons, ones not covered in her initial classes."

While the two parents turned to Cora, she confirmed, prompting the formal Amalyn to continue, "Our family, especially Tamyn, would be delighted to provide any assistance your daughter may require in her studies."

Happily, the Everstone family agreed and offered their typical, sincere gratitude.

Attempting to converse with them further, the two human parents were stopped mid-sentence when the Starborne matriarch said, "You must excuse us as we have a prior engagement we must attend to. This night, unlike most others, requires a certain attention. We shall, however, request to continue for another time. Perhaps during this week's end. We can introduce ourselves further over afternoon tea while our daughters share in their studies."

Cheerfully, Cora and her parents agreed to the invitation.

With a light nod, Amalyn appeared pleased as she concluded, "We shall have a courier sent for you, then. Tomorrow afternoon, if it pleases you."

Desiring to coordinate further, Aeyra began to seek a few more details, but was unable to as the Starborne family initiated their pace into the crowd – moving to the central section of town and aimed towards the High King's Palace.

Back to just the three, Cora and her parents were left to enjoy the remainder of the jubilee among themselves. Their agreement was to stay for as long as their little flower was not too tired. Until then, they planned to watch the rest of the festivities until they had to head home for bed.

CHAPTER TWELVE:

"A STAR'S LEGACY"

As the early afternoon began to roll in on the day after the jubilee, Aeyra and Cehdric scrambled within their home.

Shouting from one room towards her, Cehdric asked, "Where's my comb?"

Responding just as loudly, Aeyra said, "Atop the stand, our room." Moving to a more frantic tone, she continued, "I can't find my left shoe."

"Have you checked under our bed?" inquired Cehdric.

"Right," said Aeyra as she ran off to look. As she knelt down to find it hidden above the dust collected underneath the mattress, she went on, "And Cora." Speaking louder, she carried her voice, "Honey, are you ready?"

Walking up to her calmly and rested, Cora answered, "Yes, Momma."

As she put on her shoe while sitting atop the bed, Aeyra inspected her daughter – fixing her dress and pulling the few strands of golden hair back with the rest.

"There," Aeyra said as she finished. "We're all set." Calling across to him, she said, "Cehdric?"

"I'm ready as well," he responded. Joining his family atop the mattress in their room, he said in a jolly manner, "And now, we wait."

Somewhat restlessly, the Everstone family remained in the larger bedroom, but not before moving to the forward area in hopes of hearing the door sooner. They were anxious and their nerves were getting the best of them as they wondered how it would be to visit a formal, High Elf household – one they were not accustomed to as the few elves in their former village were simple, peaceful farmers like them.

Minutes seemed to last for hours, and just as they started to question if they would be called upon this day and not the next, they heard a subtle knock. Quickly, they opened the door and saw the slender, well-dressed elf that awaited.

"Greetings from the Starborne family," announced the courier with a polite bow as he slightly flung his golden, embroidered hood forward. "If it pleases you, you have been summoned to attend afternoon tea at their home. Should you require a moment to ready yourselves, I will kindly await outside."

Before the elf could turn away, Aeyra said, "No, we're ready. Where do we go?"

"You can follow me, my lady," answered the elf.

After closing the door behind them, the Everstone family proceeded alongside the cordial High Elf down the city streets of the northeast section that were still being cleaned up from the previous day's festival. Although he clearly had no fault in the matter, the elven messenger still offered his apologies for the mess while they made their way out of the northeast section and into the inner city areas.

Moving towards the High King's Palace, the family began to wonder if they were visiting with royalty and if they would see the inside of the grand castle. Yet, they passed by it and kept moving onward to the southwestern part of town.

Passing its guarded gate, the Everstones saw what seemed to be the most lavishly decorated homes within the capital. In awe, they gazed at the wonderful decorations and designs that were much larger than their simpler home.

"Quite a sight," commented Cehdric.

Returning the remark while he led, the elf said, "Indeed. This city section is predominantly where the elder families of our culture reside."

While the High Elf courier furthered on a brief portion of their history as he led them along, the Everstone family intently listened. His words made the walk seem much shorter than it likely was as within a short time, they reached the end of their journey.

Pointing at the grandiose home in front of him, the elf said, "We have arrived."

After motioning them forward, the elven courier departed – leaving the Everstone family at the front steps of the elegant home.

As the two parents each held their child by one of her hands, they made their way forward to the engraved door. Although they felt a slight nervousness within them, they did not hesitate to politely knock on the adorned frame.

Opening in an instant as if they had arrived just on time, the heavy door moved inward – revealing the inviting matriarch of the house.

"Good afternoon and welcome," greeted Amalyn with a proper curtsy. While motioning them all inwards, she said, "Please, come inside."

Before stepping past the threshold of the door, the three guests lightly stomped their feet outside to prevent tracking any debris from the streets that were still being cleaned up. Although they were concerned with not soiling the door's entranceway, the Starborne mother requested again that they come in and not to burden themselves with any dirt.

Acting as they were bid, the three then entered fully into the large forward room of the home – all wondering how it looked even bigger on the inside. The luxurious furniture and extravagant decorations, even the lush rugs atop the marbled floor, all caught their eye. Visibly, they were stunned – awed entirely by the beauty of each design.

Noticing the family that admired their dwelling, Amalyn said, "This was once my mother and father's home, they put quite a bit of care into it when times were simpler."

As she ushered her guests more inside, Amalyn pointed to the adorned stairway while announcing her entering daughter. Joining her child's side, they led the Everstones through a brief tour of their downstairs rooms, then stopped near the grand dining area that joined the elongated kitchen.

Preparing a last set of ceramic cups, the Starborne patriarch finished his task, then united with his family while saying, "Our sincerest apologies for our hasty departure yesterday evening. Rest assured, that will not be the case this afternoon."

Speaking to Tamyn, Amalyn said, "Would you care to show Miss Everstone your room, then the study where you shall be helping her with the lessons?"

Cordially, Tamyn nodded her head, then motioned for her friend to come.

Looking up at her parents, Cora first sought their approval. As they happily agreed, she let go of their hands, then extended her hand outwards to Tamyn.

Shying away at first, Tamyn stared oddly at her young friend, then grabbed her awkwardly after her mother said towards the innocent child, "Go on, dear."

As their children went upstairs, the four adults stayed among one another with watchful smiles.

Being the first to break the silence, the elven father said while turning to Aeyra and Cehdric, "Seems I must apologize again in having forsaken my manners. Allow me to introduce myself, I am Thuriel Elderpine, Tamyn's father."

Responding in kind to the elven patriarch, Cora's parents shared a formal greeting, but did so with a slightly raised eyebrow at first – one they made sure to polish away quickly.

Having noticed the expression, Thuriel furthered, "I am familiar with that look, rest assured." As the Everstones tried to apologize, he went on, "Please, there is no need to concern and I take no offense. I agree, it is odd for a daughter and a mother to not take her father's name as it is not tradition." Gazing over to his wife with affection, he said, "Deep down, I know she would have, yet I refused to be the end of such a great family name for our people and so, I requested the High King make the exception." Attempting to lighten the mood, he added, "And the gods know I would not want your father haunting my dreams if you took the name."

Although he tried a cheerful remark, Amalyn visibly grew slightly flustered as she turned her cheek away while a set of tears formed in her eyes. Wiping them off quickly, she turned and said, "My apologies, this time of year is never quite as easy." Referring to the recent jubilee, she went on, "The war took quite the toll on our family."

As Aeyra and Cehdric offered their condolences for their loss, Amalyn said, "Please, please." After a light sniff to hold back further sentiment, she continued, "Let us speak over tea, if you would not mind joining us."

Guiding the agreeing family over to the dining table that was already set with a silver-colored kettle alongside bejeweled utensils, Amalyn and Thuriel pulled their chairs out to allow their visitors to take a seat first. As the Everstone parents settled themselves, the two elves assisted one another in pouring the floral-scented, steamy liquid into the fine, ceramic cups. After adding honey and sugar to their guests' desires, they then took a seat after pouring some for themselves.

After a few sips of the hot beverage, Thuriel offered an array of biscuits to all – assorted from sweet to tart. As the human wife and husband picked out just a few, he offered several suggestions and bid they take as many as they like.

"Please, feel as if you are at home," said Thuriel.

"Yes, please," joined Amalyn with a cheerful expression. Watching as they enjoyed the delights they offered, she continued, "Anything for a family that has been exceptionally kind to our daughter."

Taking one more sip of tea to warm her insides, Amalyn lowered her cup to its small plate, then elaborated, "She has had quite a lot of undue pressure on her since she was born, mostly due to her name. Her outlet has been reservation and a certain hesitation with others, which we have begun to see fade the moment she befriended your Cora."

"Our little tulip's quite charming," bragged Cehdric.

Correcting her husband's remark, Aeyra said in a less boastful tone, "Cora's always been kind, caring, and generous. We're very proud of her."

"As you should be," said Amalyn with sincerity. "She is also quite intelligent as I gather, although disadvantaged having come into such an advanced class at her age."

Seeing the slight worry grow onto the face of Aeyra and Cehdric, she felt the urge to explain. "The courses given to the High Elves are meant to be challenging," said Amalyn. "Much of what your daughter would have been taught, had she stayed with Instructor Pepperton, refers to the history and cultural heritage many of us were imparted with in earlier schooling before magister training. She is going through an entirely new curriculum, one she has never prepared for."

Feeling the most concerned as he had not received the same explanation from the Arch Magister, Cehdric asked, "Shouldn't we be worried it'll be too hard for her?"

"Not anymore, I assure you," answered Amalyn. "Behind our daughter's reserved nature lies an overconfident, highly skilled student. She has had twice the amount of schooling before entering training than her peers and is not only qualified, but willing to tutor your daughter."

Offering their gratitude, the Everstone family smiled and grew overjoyed. As she and her husband received their thanks, Amalyn said, "Once more, it is we who should be grateful. Tamyn is one year shy of thirty, she has been teased by those around her for being an almost fully grown adult in a first year class as her fellows are only just leaving adolescence. Your Cora has lifted her spirits and brought our daughter back from isolation."

"And your daughter's been a blessing as well," added Aeyra. "We've noticed a slight hesitancy towards school the last few days, but they've seemed to fade with her newfound friendship."

Joining in, Thuriel said with a modest, but delighted tone, "Seems we are both in debt to one another."

"Yes," nodded Amalyn to her husband. While taking another sip of her tea, then putting it back down, she grew slightly stern towards him and continued, "However, it is up to us to do as much as we can, considering our position."

Bobbing his head up, then holding it down, Thuriel agreed. Adjusting herself back to face the human parents, Amalyn furthered, "As close friends of the Arch Magister, we support the decision you have made, one we feel was best for your daughter." As Cora's parents looked to one another, she continued, "Rest assured, we know of what ails her. It was shared to us in private as our daughter has a similar gift to your own."

"If you can help us with that, anything," begged Aeyra with a slightly distraught voice, "we'd be eternally grateful."

While caressing his wife, Cehdric said, "We've been so worried, it's getting worse."

Expressing greater concern, Aeyra opened up her emotions while saying, "She's even seeing part of some battle now. We need to know what to do before she gets hurt."

Attempting to comfort the two, Amalyn offered as she leaned in closer, "The best course is to do as Astrael has suggested – to train her. With her help, and ours, Cora will be well."

Pulling back and grabbing a napkin as if expecting to wipe something off, Amalyn said, "Quite ironic, it seems though. You wish to part with that which I would give anything to see." Catching the intrigue of Cora's parents, she explained with a growing mournfulness, "It is not just any battle she sees, but the one that claimed my father before the war's end." Wiping a tear off her lid, she continued after a brief sniffle, "To see him just one more time."

While holding his wife, Cehdric asked, "Your father was part of this 'Baydyn's Gambit'?"

As Thuriel consoled her softly, Amalyn responded, "Baydyn was my father, the High General of our combined armies in the great war."

"I-I'm sorry," offered Cehdric. "We didn't know, we're just gardeners and farmers in Riverbend – we never studied any…"

Raising his hand gently upwards, Thuriel eased the apologetic father and confirmed they took no offense. Despite his words, Cehdric, and soon Aeyra, continued to express their remorse for their lack of knowledge.

Attempting to divert the matter and provide insight into their daughter's visions, Amalyn interjected, "You are probably wondering why Cora is witnessing these particular events and what they mean."

Inhaling deeply, Amalyn readied herself to recall her father's final moments. "You see," she started with an exhale, "we were losing ground in the war. The southern lines of Arulan barely held, while the northern, and eventually the western lands in Vjord were lost completely. As their last stronghold in the west was razed, my father had a choice – to scurry to our borders and reinforce them, or protect our human allies in the north along with the many undefended villages and refugees that would surely be left for slaughter. His selflessness," she gulped, "is what saved us all."

As she cleaned off the lone droplet that started to run down her cheek, Amalyn continued, "He used the enemy's greed to lure out their entire northern force to the south and into a trap – with simply a golden chest carried by him and his twelve best on horseback. The enemy was intended to believe it to be one of our twelve artifacts being sent in secret to our northwestern border, yet they were sorely mistaken. As they assailed my father and reached the empty chest at the Sunford Fields within our lands; the combined might of the

Shimmering Fort to the west, the High King from the south, and the Vjordic peoples along with my father's remaining force from the northeast fell upon them. It was the very event that turned the tide to our favor before the war's end."

As the others listened intently, Amalyn went on, "As far as what she sees, we do not have the details of what occurred in the time between Astrael departing my father's company in her grave state and before the larger battle began. Your daughter may yet be receiving an insight from the gods themselves as to those lost events."

Asking passionately, Aeyra said, "Have they no mercy on an innocent mind? To put her through so much at such a young age?"

"We may never know the reason," answered Amalyn with hope towards the mother. "Yet, we do know their burden can be lessened dramatically, even completely once she finds what they want her to see."

As their front door unexpectedly knocked, the conversation was briefly interrupted as Thuriel excused himself to attend to it.

Staying with Aeyra and Cehdric, Amalyn furthered her thought, "Time and proper training are your daughter's best allies in this. It is what helped our own Tamyn, and even those few before who have been chosen with such a responsibility."

Returning with a slight urgency, Thuriel apologized for his brief absence and said, "I regret to do this once more, yet it seems there is a sudden matter we must attend to." As Amalyn looked at him in confusion, he clarified, "Some odd occurrences in the deeper south again, nothing to worry over – just needs to be addressed is all."

Begrudgingly, Amalyn agreed, but not before turning over to Aeyra and Cehdric. "If you would permit," she asked, "could you please consider letting Tamyn join you back home for the remainder of the afternoon – that is, to continue tutoring your daughter."

"Of course," said Aeyra as both she and her husband agreed. "We'd be happy to have her over."

"And we would be delighted to have one of our couriers send you an evening meal," added Thuriel. "One prepared by the High King's own cooks."

Furthering his proposal, Amalyn added, "Should you require anything at all, please do not hesitate. Our considerable resources are always available to those who do well by our family and act for the good of our people."

"We're but humble workers with no desires but our daughter's well-being and safety," returned Cehdric as he graciously denied any compensation along with his wife.

As they all then stood to give each other a farewell, Aeyra leaned in an upward motion and embraced the Starborne matriarch that was a few inches shy of her own husband's height. "Thank you," she offered again in clear appreciation. "Both your family and the Arch Magister have shown us a great kindness." After pulling back from the hug, she atoned for her burst of emotions and finished, "We appreciate all you're doing for our little flower."

CHAPTER THIRTEEN:

"JUST A STICK"

Seemingly, the week's end passed with such speed that before Cora knew it, she was already returning to class. She was accompanied by others who arrived into Ravenbeak's room on time – some appearing enthused to begin the day's lesson, while others looked visibly tired from a lack of rest likely due to the festival's celebrations.

Making her way down the aisle, Cora noticed that Tamyn had already arrived and even taken her seat before her. Although she was excited to see her friend, Tamyn was clearly more so as her morning greeting was uttered just prior to the hand wave Cora initiated.

Joining in on the cheerful, early welcome, Cora said a few words until she realized all others around her were far quieter – causing her to hop silently into her desk to await the Instructor's announcements.

As a few minutes passed, the remainder of the students quietly assumed their seats and Ravenbeak then stepped forward from his chair. Before initiating his usual statements that started his day, he called forth Mister Spearhawk and Miss Bronzehelm – the front two students of the left and center aisles. Pointing the duo outwards, he did so while informing them to assist their special guest for the upcoming lesson.

As the pair of pupils made their exit, Instructor Ravenbeak said, "I do hope that this morning you have all returned rested and prepared following the jubilee, for there will be as always, a substantial amount to cover."

After opening with a few morning topics, the two students soon returned with a third High Elf that paused the Instructor. Although most appeared to focus on the entering elf's armor or his light eyes and hair, Cora set her gaze onto the two-headed dragon pin he wore – one similar to what she was used to seeing in her visions.

Despite her being struck in awe for different reasons, all other students joined her as they appeared to be drawn in a mild fascination to the three decorated crates that were brought in and set to rest atop a table Instructor Ravenbeak had previously set.

After the younger pair returned to their desks, the Instructor continued with the armored elf alongside him. "Our exercise for today will be rather different," he said while turning to the fellow elder next to him, then back to the class. "Although I am quite capable of providing the training, we have been required to accommodate a unique guest for this lecture. Please grant him your undivided attention and be sure to have your attunement gems ready when they are called for." Looking back towards Cora, he stressed, "I do hope you have all kept them safe over the week's end and not misplaced them." Shifting back towards the armored elf, he finished his presentation, "Without further delay, I present to you the Highguard Second of his contingent within the Shimmering Fort, Caspen Morrowbloom."

Clapping briefly, the class welcomed the Highguard soldier, then stopped all sounds as he said, "A gracious introduction, Instructor." With a hint of sarcasm, he carried on, "You have my utmost gratitude and certainly that of the Head Instructor for making arrangements on such a short notice in Magister Duskwallow's absence."

Taking a step forward, Caspen addressed towards the class, "Yet rest assured, you are in more than capable hands this morning as I was once an Instructor of The School prior to being a battle-tested magister." Offering a light bow that was aimed specifically towards Tamyn, he followed, "I offer you my sincerest greetings for allowing me to teach you this morning."

Despite the mildly sour face of Instructor Ravenbeak, Caspen continued without interruption as he lifted his head up and said, "As was stated of me, I am a member of the Highguard. I am not here to speak to you this day on your recruitment – of our prestigious ranks or the other assignments within the Grand Sanctum and its outlying libraries – as that is for a later year. Rather, I come to you today as one of few who is considered to be not only a highly proficient user, but also a craftsman and repairer of wands. Or, at least my superiors would have me believe."

As some quietly cracked a smile at the light jest, Caspen began unveiling the boxed contents of that which he brought. Displaying several wands made of amber-yew, oak, ebonwood, and other fine materials with varying colors, he went on, "For the remainder of the morning, we shall be going over the functionality, use, and even assignment of this weapon to the gems you have chosen or been chosen by."

Raising his hand first after a somewhat sour stare towards Tamyn, Deverin asked after being called upon. "Instructor. Highguard Morrowbloom," he said. "Can we not insert our gem into perhaps a sword or staff of our choosing instead?"

While Instructor Ravenbeak visibly grinned in delight towards the question, the veteran magister replied. "As you progress in your training, you may choose as you desire based on your preferences, even discard your gem for another if you like. Yet for those of you in your first year, you must first learn the wand before all else."

"Highguard Morrowbloom," said Deverin in a follow-up inquiry that was clearly encouraged by Ravenbeak, "why must we first practice with the 'weapon' of a novice before a more functional one?"

Although he was being clearly mocked by a student that appeared to be one of Ravenbeak's favorites, Caspen calmly responded, "If you would not mind, I can demonstrate if you step forward."

After receiving smiles from Varissa and Ravenbeak, Deverin stood to join Magister Caspen at the front of the class. To appear more than capable, he stood with his chest arched forward and arms to his side – posing robustly as he awaited the guest instructor.

Picking out a random wand, Caspen handed the stick that was nearly a foot in length to the pupil, then said, "You seem naturally adept, I want you to motion as you would when casting a spell."

Winding himself back, Deverin moved his arm in a fluid rotation around his head and lunged it forward. His move seemed elegant and clearly rehearsed, even studied – an action that clearly impressed Ravenbeak and Varissa who nodded in approval.

"Too simple," boasted Deverin who obviously felt the task was beneath him.

"Indeed," said Caspen who eloquently grabbed the wand back and returned it to its display. "Yet, had that been a staff or sword, your mighty swing would have knocked someone's head or cut it right off while you train within the classroom." Grabbing his own worn wand off his belt, he did a simple flick, then continued, "This is the motion required of most spells you will learn throughout your first year. You are initiates, not masters of your craft who will be summoning whirlwinds or firestorms."

Turning back around and gripping a half dozen wands, Caspen then clumped them tightly with both hands. Facing towards Deverin, he said, "Strength is clearly your attribute. A powerful student such as yourself should easily be able to break these fragile weapons. Do so, and I shall personally see to imbuing a sword worthy of your might with the gem you carry. Fail, and I ask you to resume your seat in silence for the remainder of the lesson."

Opening his palms to receive the tight bundle being laid down onto them, Deverin commented, "These sticks are weak, are you certain you want me to break them?"

"Indeed," said Caspen with a smirk. "They can be repaired, even after being easily split in half by one so mighty."

Following a shrug, Deverin said, "Very well."

Twisting his hands firmly around the wands, Deverin held them closely, then started to push harshly. As the wooden weapons held, he put more force – even straining his face and using his knee to assist his strained hands. No matter how hard he tried, they did not break or even crack.

Seeing the exhausted student who attempted for nearly a minute, Caspen reached in and grabbed the wands from

Deverin's reddened palms. While pointing the pupil to his seat and reminding him to keep quiet, he placed his wands back into their crates – leaving only his own within his grip.

Watching as the magister trainee sat, Caspen moved his wand in front of his chest and said, "The strength of these, like many weapons, are not in its size, but in its unity. Magister formations in combat are just as unbreakable as this bundle when held together." Swishing his wand around, he continued, "The same can be said of a sword and a spear, yet to truly harness magic we must cast and aim a spell. These larger and often hindering weapons may force you to be separate of others or even alone entirely to avoid injuring one of your own. We Highguards, just like those of you in The School, train and function best as a combined unit – protecting and relying on one another as a whole, not as individuals.

"Our ranks," Caspen continued while initiating a pace around the front part of the room, "are comprised of those with sword, shield, spear, and bow – ones whose expertise in these weapons spans for even centuries." Lifting up his wand, he followed, "Yet, in this tiny 'stick', lies all those armaments and more – harnessing the very flame, wind, or water and earth used to forge them." Turning to the silent Deverin, he finished, "However, I do not aim to discourage you and those others who feel otherwise as there are compatriots of mine, even those close to me, who feel safest when carrying their own blade. Yet for me, this is the only weapon I will ever require and it, too, is the same for you during this first year of training where you shall attempt to master it."

Encouraging the class to rise after concluding a portion of his lecture, Highguard Morrowbloom requested they all come up to the large table in front.

As her peers rushed forward, Cora remained slightly behind with Tamyn – finding a spot in the rear as the rest pushed their way up.

Noticing the much shorter student, Caspen peeked over the side of the group, then said, "Come forward, my lady. You conceal yourself as one would a wand in the presence of the High King." Contrary to Ravenbeak's unsympathetic attitude towards her, the Highguard Second continued, "As we have shown earlier, there is strength in even the smallest of things that do not appear sharp or imposing. For one so young to be among us, it would honor me if you made the first selection."

Being proud of her friend, Tamyn initiated a small cheer that garnered the support of others around her, though visibly not Deverin and Varissa as they rolled their eyes at the sight. Despite their attitude, most encouraged Cora as she joyously stepped forward to gaze at the exhibit.

In front of the middle bin, she instantly eyed a simplistic white wand. Reaching in, she pulled it outward, then said, "May I have this one?"

With a smile, Highguard Morrowbloom answered, "Of course, my lady. It is a fine selection."

Contently, Caspen then looked to the rest of the students as he began to embolden them as a group to pick one of the many remaining wands in an orderly fashion.

Acting as they were told, the remainder of Ravenbeak's class sorted through the wide array of wooden weapons – from short to long, elaborate and simple. After a few moments when each had their choice, he requested they all resume their seats to move forward with his presentation.

"These wands that you will train with," Caspen said while raising his own upward, "are all fit to hold your standard attunement gem that you have each previously received." Showing them the small notch and locking grip at the tip, he resumed, "I ask you each to insert your gem, then clamp it tightly."

Walking around the room, he began to observe the students as they followed his directions. Seeing some slightly struggle, he said, "No gem is the same, you may have to adjust your locks accordingly for a better fit. Ensure it is snug and safe." Moving to the first row, he went on, "Once you are finished, please place your wand back onto your desk so that I may inspect."

Moving down each row and aisle, Highguard Morrowbloom carefully examined each wooden piece when the pupils were done. He took his time on every single one, cautiously reviewing each notch's clasping mechanism and making corrections where he saw fit before resuming his position at the head of the class.

After it was all to his satisfaction, Caspen resumed his speech, "Now that we have matched your gem to its wand, we are nearly there." Expressing himself in a pensive manner, he continued, "It will remain incomplete until it is paired with the most important element – you. Without the knowledge of magic and its words to express them, you simply hold a carved piece of wood with a shiny jewel."

Alluding towards the class' previous studies, he continued, "Over the course of the last few weeks, you have all been learning the language of the Dracozim that allows us to summon their powers, their magic. It is a partially known language, of fragments and short words that cannot even form sentences. Yet what we do know and have gathered throughout our people's history, is enough to alter the course of progress or even turn a battle with just the tiniest of words from its vocabulary."

Moving back and forth from each end of the room so as to cover each aisle, he said in an empowering manner, "It is for you, each of you, to learn, to sensibly use, and to preserve this gift that was bestowed upon us by the gods themselves. A grand responsibility that we must never forget, of maintaining the peaceful balance and not seeking to disrupt it."

Going on in a cautious voice, Caspen furthered, "History has taught us the dangers of magic's use, and with this new weapon you have received, you will be charged with ensuring its safe and proper handling while in training. Only with supervision from your Instructors within The School and under the courses you are taught will you exercise spells from the words you already know, and those you will continue to learn until your graduation."

"And continue, you shall," said Instructor Ravenbeak where the Highguard left off. Pacing near his side and not allowing the guest teacher to continue his thoughts, he addressed what he clearly felt were only his students, "You will have over the next three weeks to practice the words for the spells you have been taught, along with a specific number of others that we shall go over until the sixtieth day of fall. Then, you will each be individually evaluated for a practical assessment."

"An assessment where individual predispositions are considered, surely," added Highguard Morrowbloom as he noticed the Instructor finish his sentence with an apprehensive gaze towards where Tamyn and Cora sat. "As it is cautioned, even outlawed, to not practice certain magic outside of a student's skillset."

"It indeed is considered for all future assessments," responded Ravenbeak arrogantly as he looked down to his peer. "Yet, it will not be a concern for this evaluation. As one who has taught a first year class for quite some time, the students are only learning words bound to all schools of magic. Regardless of the skills they possess, the spells can be performed without reprisal."

Taking a step towards the slightly less full crates atop the table, Instructor Ravenbeak gave no chance for Highguard Morrowbloom to resume his lesson as he asked the two initial students – Mister Spearhawk and Miss Bronzehelm – to rise once more and assist, but this time on Caspen's exit.

"Please," said Ravenbeak sarcastically, "let us all give the Highguard Second a gracious farewell for his time and speech as our morning guest." Further jabbing at him while acting slightly resentful, he added, "We will be sure to give our thanks as well to the Head Instructor for allowing you to be a part of our curriculum for this portion of the day."

Maintaining his pride and calm nature, Caspen nodded his head in kind to the feigned manners provided by the bitter Instructor who did the same. While lifting himself up after a slight bow, Caspen offered to the pupils of his class a sincere statement of gratefulness coupled with a kind farewell. Shifting lastly towards Ravenbeak, he then concluded before making his leave with a grin, "I will be certain to give your regards to the Head Instructor. Please, be sure to share mine as well with the Grand Magister."

CHAPTER FOURTEEN:

"RECALLING THE FORGOTTEN"

S trolling into the halls with a jittery sensation in her hands and stomach, Cora entered The School with a slight anxiety that had been building up over the last three weeks. With each passing day, she grew closer to the exam that she could not help but mull over incessantly.

In her state of worry, Cora started to recite some of her previous lessons in class while including bits from her extracurricular study sessions with her elven friend, Tamyn. Walking by the usual classes, then her room's door, and into her seat, she seemingly ignored all else as she went on recalling what she had been taught.

As Cora sat down, Tamyn easily felt her peer's nervousness as she said, "Must be a real concern of yours if you have not the mind for anything else."

"I-I'm sorry," muttered Cora as she raised her head towards her friend. "I should've said good morning, I'm just so worried about us passing this test."

Grabbing her own text, Tamyn then turned back to Cora and placed the bulky book onto her desk. Opening a page marked on its edge, Tamyn asked, "Do you remember this spell?" As Cora nodded, she moved to another line, then resumed, "And this one?"

When her human friend bobbed her head up and down several more times in acknowledgement after a few more incantation paragraphs were pointed out, Tamyn said, "Do you see? You need not overstress, you are prepared."

"I guess," mumbled Cora. Concerned with how the last examination snuck up on her, she said, "But what if we're asked different questions?"

Blinking her eyes with a light shrug, Tamyn responded, "It is always uncertain what we will be asked to perform. Yet, the Instructor cannot stray much from what we have learned in these texts and he will only be evaluating us on these general spells. He will not, for example, be asking you to perform any fire incantations while knowing your gifts lie in water as it is outlawed and punishable to teach in such a way." Still sensing some slight concern on her friend, she furthered, "Yet, if it worries you such, we can continue to study over the next few days until our assessment to ensure we both succeed."

With the examination's burden lessened by her older friend, Cora began to smile and expressed her gratitude as she said, "Yes, please. Thank you. I'll ask Momma and Poppa if you could visit again or I can go over. I'm sure they won't mind either."

As they were focused on their exchange with one another, Tamyn and Cora did not notice the Instructor standing while the rest of the class silenced themselves in preparation for the coming day's lesson. They continued their planning for after school studies until the Instructor strolled up to their row in the aisle. When they caught the perturbed look on Ravenbeak's face, they both turned forward, but it was too late.

"No, no," said the Instructor sarcastically. "Please, do go on. What you were speaking of is clearly far more important than my lesson plan." Swinging around to face the rest of the class, he bellowed, "Do you hear, class? Our two most disruptive students clearly have more pressing matters than this curriculum."

Although Cora bashfully tucked her head in with embarrassment to hide her rosy cheeks, Tamyn remained firm and tall – sitting upright in a prideful manner that only provoked the Instructor more.

Going on in an agitated manner, Ravenbeak said aloud, "Perhaps it is because Miss Starborne and her little friend feel they know this course better than the rest and do not need the preparation I was going to offer for the practical assessment that is coming up in three days." Picking up Tamyn's book off of Cora's desk, he continued towards her, "Seems Miss Starborne does not even require her own text. Her 'advanced' studies are clearly superior to the rest of the class, so she will not be needing it until the examination passes."

Having her book confiscated, Tamyn observed without a flinch, but added a whisper, "I have more at home."

Growing furious with the comment, the Instructor lashed out in a much louder manner, "I am certain of it, as one of privilege would." Lunging towards the basket under Cora's desk, he snatched her textbook and further said, "Yet, one who has no more than the tattered clothes she wears surely does not."

As Cora cried out and began to beg, Tamyn comforted her by saying, "Do not worry, I have our notes at home and even spare books for you."

Laughing angrily at the pair, Ravenbeak crossed his arms and said, "Clearly, you do not need my instruction then. As you are obviously far more prepared than any other, you will perform a demonstration for the class this morning." Staring at Tamyn, he harshly added, "So get up."

Being forced to rise, Tamyn slammed her hands onto her desk, then pushed herself upwards aggressively. Looking fiercely towards the Instructor, she asked, "What sort of spell would you care to see? One that teaches patience, or perhaps understanding?"

"Front!" yelled the Instructor. "Now!" Watching as Tamyn marched forward, he continued, "Move it!"

Keeping her eyes on both her friend and the teacher, Cora watched as the Instructor took out his own wand. As he then aimed it at Tamyn, she screamed aloud, "Watch out!"

Stopping her pace, Tamyn turned around as the Instructor made his incantation request. "Shield," he said towards her while simultaneously lighting up his own wand with a spark.

Responding as fast as she could, Tamyn took the brown, cedar wand off her garments, then slashed it upwards while reciting, "Hildaest!"

Forming a brief, protective bubble in front of her, Tamyn barely blocked the light bolt that was sent hurling towards her.

Clearly desiring to harm his student, Ravenbeak in his frustration called out a harsher strike, uttering the word, "Secarith."

With a slightly larger enchantment flying towards her, Tamyn used her shielding spell once more in an attempt to absorb the blow. Despite being more ready for it, however, her buffer shattered and caused her extended hand a mild pain.

While his student grabbed her ailing wrist, Ravenbeak furthered while still pointing his wand outward, "Detawlamh."

As the burst struck, Tamyn's wand was sent from her right hand and onto the floor next to her. Opening her mouth, she began to yell out at the Instructor, but was silenced completely when he stepped forward and said, "Naciuin."

Unable to speak and without her weapon, Tamyn was left helpless and alone at the front of the class as the Instructor kept pacing towards her.

Arrogantly, Ravenbeak began to brag, "It seems you were not as prepared as you thought you were." Putting his wand back onto his belt, he continued to berate her as he said, "Perhaps you would care to admit your misguided manners and allow me to instruct the class?"

Moving her lips but with no words coming out, Tamyn kept trying in frustration to respond but was unable to. As she tried, Ravenbeak said, "Very well, another example then."

Shifting his body towards the last seat in his room, Ravenbeak looked at Cora then said, "Miss Everstone, if you would care to join us."

Shaking her head frantically in a fearful manner, Cora said, "Please, no. I'm, I-I can't."

Pushing her further to stand up, the Instructor said, "You can and you shall." Seeing that she still sat while fervently pleading, he began to march towards her but stopped when she stepped out of her desk.

"Please," Cora continued as a few tears formed in her eyes.

Looking at her ailing friend, Cora kept on reiterating and begging, but it did not appear to do much to change the Instructor's mind as he said, "A simple spell. If you cannot even show us that, then I may as well fail you for the assessment already."

Feeling as if she had no choice, Cora begrudgingly made her way down the aisle and towards Tamyn while clutching her wand in both hands. Concerned with her friend, she tried to help her, but was denied as Tamyn silently postured herself to instead protect Cora.

"Now, Miss Starborne," said the Instructor. "You already had your turn, please allow Miss Everstone." While his student stood firm in a protective manner, he added, "I assure you, her task shall be much simpler. All I ask is she purge you of that which halts your speech before its effects wear off." Putting his hands behind his back and away from his wand, he insisted, "Which by my estimate, should be shortly."

Gazing towards her friend, Tamyn allowed Cora to step forward after providing her a nod of confidence – one the entire class could see. Putting her hand onto her lowered shoulders, she quietly tried to lift up Cora's spirits with an encouraging nudge.

"I-I'll do it," stuttered Cora as she wiped her reddened face and looked up to her tall, elven friend. "I can do it."

Gripping her wand with her right hand first, then with both, she pointed it out towards Tamyn and aimed it near her throat. Closing her eyes, she concentrated herself, then said, "Fae, umm, Faeluget."

Even though her lids were closed, Cora could see the small light that emanated in front of her as she concurrently heard Tamyn utter, "I…"

Letting out a smile, Cora began to open her eyes proudly to see the effects of the curative spell she cast, but to her dismay, Tamyn was gone.

Wondering what had occurred, Cora stared up and around, but instead of her classroom, she found a blinding beam of sunlight as it pierced through a series of clouds. In the Instructor's place, another male voice took over as he said to her bewilderment, "I will stand until the very end, shoulder-to-shoulder with those I am proud to fight alongside."

Turning towards the sound, Cora saw the same grassy hill and the six armored High Elves that she had become familiar with in her visions. Shocked and letting out a loud gasp, she could only silently observe in her motionless state as the other five lifted up the one they called the High General.

Having been struck by an arrow into his leg, the High General limped and struggled, but still stood next to those of his kin that were just as wounded as he. With arrowheads and shafts covering their shields and the ground surrounding them, the six elves moved to formation with their leader at the forefront. Drawing their swords out, they held tightly as the ground trembled and menacing roars echoed all around them.

As they readied for what seemed to be an overwhelming enemy, the armored elves suddenly became surprised as all sounds around them stopped – even the quaking earth from the rushing legions.

With all noise gone, all that Cora and the nearby High Elves heard was the screech of a vulture, followed by a hissing noise.

Still prepared for the enemy, the elves did not let up their defenses and faced the top of the hill as they awaited what would come from it. Although Cora was nervous and in clear fright, the battered elves were not as they valiantly maintained their guarded stance with their remaining might.

Anxiously, Cora peeked onto the hilltop as the others did – waiting for the lone pair of footsteps that now became apparent in its approach. Frightened and worried, she began

144

to quiver, then cowered into a ball as the top of a dark hood started to bounce over from the other side.

Unlike the courageous elves that dauntlessly stood firm, Cora was stunned and unable to move – even helpless to look away at the top of the ashy cloak that bounced forward as goosebumps covered her skin.

Suddenly and to Cora's astonishment, the approaching figure stopped. To the north and just in front of her, the sky unexpectedly darkened and blotted out most of the sun. As a gloomy aura began to set itself over the hill, both she and the elves could feel an eerie sensation building – one they were unable to shake.

Hearing a mysterious, frightening whisper from all around the hill, they all felt a chill as a rush of wind started to encircle their position. Winding itself up into a swirling cloud of black and silver, the darkness rushed upwards, then harshly down to all that stood below it.

Loudly, Cora let out a tear-filled scream at its imposing sight – one that was muffled by the sounds from the High Elves that were visibly pained by its effects. As the cloud grew darker and moved faster, the noise became deafening to Cora as its gust was all she could hear. With her ears ringing, all her senses began to fade but her sight as she could only see the grey storm and a bright red glow that emanated from the center of it.

Seeking a way out of the dark whirlwind, the only action she could think of was closing her eyes while yelling out, "Help! Please, let me go back home!"

While she scrunched her eyelids and shook in terror, all Cora could feel was a warm embrace followed by the familiar voice of Tamyn as she said, "You are here, safe. See for yourself."

Blinking as a few droplets fell down her cheek, Cora looked up to notice she had once again fallen but was clearly caught by Tamyn. Frantically, she moved herself away from her friend and began to gaze around.

"The cloud, the dark cloud," she said. "I saw it, it was all around hurting everyone."

"Cora," said Tamyn reassuringly as she grabbed a hold of her friend that felt cold to the touch. "There is nothing here." Forcing her to look up at the ceiling and then the walls, she reaffirmed, "See? Only our classroom."

Although Tamyn attempted to calm her panicked friend, Ravenbeak interrupted as he moved towards them.

"Well," he said, "seems Miss Everstone may yet be ready for her assessment after all." Without a care for his human student, he continued, "Now if you would please cease your little act and return to your seats, it would be appreciated." While Tamyn held the unmoving Cora, he reiterated, "Go on, before I expel you both again from this class."

As he paced right by the pair and moved to the front of the room, Ravenbeak added, "And do not think of taking her to the infirmary this time as she did not fall on her head." As he mockingly grinned towards Cora, he furthered, "Although, her hysteria would make it appear she did."

Angered by the statement but concerned for her friend, Tamyn restrained herself and did what she felt was best for the two by returning to their desks. She paid no attention to the unsympathetic Instructor, even Deverin and Varissa who pointed and chuckled at her. Calmly while blocking all else, she set Cora down first and provided a set of reassuring words, then resumed her own seat after a fellow student passed her wand down the aisle.

When Tamyn settled herself in, Instructor Ravenbeak did not hesitate to begin his announcement. "Now that we are all calm and silent," he said, "we may begin." Sternly looking towards his two, obviously least favorite students, he continued, "Discipline, although not covered by this curriculum, must clearly be taught and reinforced here. Due to Miss Starborne and Miss Everstone's outburst and disruption, our lesson for the day shall be altered."

Moving to his board, Ravenbeak said, "Rather than receive additional study materials and practice for your upcoming assessment, you shall all write lines for the remainder of the morning and the afternoon."

As the students' faces grew displeased, Ravenbeak furthered in a manner that would clearly garner hostility towards Cora and Tamyn. "All books and notes," he said more fervently, "shall be put away. In its place, you shall only take out five sheets of parchment." Initiating a composition on the board with his dark chalk, he continued "On it, you shall write 'Disrupting Instructor Ravenbeak's lessons shall not be tolerated' on the front and back side."

Underlining the words that he wrote while in his agitated state, the Instructor turned around to stare at the class as he concluded, "You can all thank Miss Starborne and Miss Everstone for the remainder of the morning until we break for our mandatory lunch, to which then a new disciplinary phrase shall await you in the afternoon."

In a bitter manner, Instructor Ravenbeak then sat down onto his chair while staring at Tamyn and Cora as they both began to take out the writing paper and instruments unhappily like the rest of the class did.

CHAPTER FIFTEEN:

"LESSER ELF"

Her belly was less than full and her soft breath hinted of the savory delights she just barely had the appetite to consume. Although her mouth let out a few gasps, Cora kept it mostly shut – silent as part of their punishment.

With her head low, she was quietly making her way back into the classroom at the end of the tall line while following the other dozen classmates that did the same. Unenthusiastically, she soon paced inside and right past the parchment board that spelled out the morning discipline her class had received. Not seeking further reprisal, she looked away as she walked right past the Instructor who awaited intently at the front of the room with their imminent afternoon assignment – one he clearly devised over the lunch period.

Continuing to be ushered inward by the line of students that went before her, Cora followed closely. She went past the first aisle, then the second, and finally to the last where she sat. Staring at the floor and her short steps, she went down the rows solemnly and peeked up only slightly at the fourth to share a saddened look with Tamyn, who was just taking to her desk with a disgruntled face that hinted at her visible anger towards the Instructor.

Although Cora felt the inner desire to speak with her friend about what she had recently witnessed, she knew it would result in further repercussions towards them. Instead, she gazed back down to her feet while continuing on with the few remaining steps to her chair. Reluctantly, she then hopped on and waited with her head down – only staring at the five sheets of parchment that were covered in ink from the lines she had just written on them.

In a pensive and sorrowful state, Cora soon began reflecting on her latest vision atop her desk and mulled over the frightening sight she wished would go away. Already worried, she was easily startled from her somber thoughts when the Instructor firmly threw the classroom door shut, then called aloud.

"I do hope you have had quite an enjoyable lunch," he said amid the displeased stares, "as the remainder of the afternoon will be far less delightful." Without wasting any time, Ravenbeak grabbed his dark chalk stick and began to write out a new series of words atop his large, parchment board.

Vigorously, the Instructor continued on with his sentence – cracking some of the stick's end and letting loose its dust with each letter he marked. He sought nothing else but to spell out his castigation, but was halted when the door to his right unexpectedly flung open.

Wasting no time in announcing herself, the perturbed Head Instructor made her entrance and harshly said towards her subordinate, "Limrich, a word in my office."

As he was commanded forward by his superior, Ravenbeak lowered his chalk, then took a step and said, "Head Instructor, can it not wait a moment?"

"No," responded the visibly frustrated matriarch of The School. Pointing past the frame she stood by, she demanded, "Outside, now."

Pulled into the hallway to speak of a clearly pressing matter by his elder, Instructor Ravenbeak had no choice but to leave the students unattended as the door was vigorously closed behind him.

Although most remained quiet, Varissa took it upon herself to make the first comment in a low voice. "Well," she said, "seems we may rest our hands for some time."

Gazing right at his peer, Deverin followed her and said, "I concur." Continuing on while looking around to the rest of the class, he added, "Yet, this would appear to be a wasted opportunity if we did not express our gratitude for this mess." Motioning for all to stare at Tamyn and Cora, he went on spouting sarcastically, "Truly, thank you for continuing to be so troublesome. We look forward to receiving punishments for the remainder of the year on your behalf."

As a small number of the class was incited to speak out, Cora felt a slight regret of talking during the morning announcements. While an uneasy sensation of guilt settled itself in her stomach, she tucked into her desk and said, "Please, I'm sorry."

"Sorry?" laughed Varissa.

Joining her, Deverin added, "An apology will not help us pass this assessment or make it any easier." As the rest of the class listened in on his speech, he continued, "What are you going to do to correct this? Or rather, what shall we do to get even?"

"Nothing," followed Tamyn, who raised her voice amid the other students'. "It is not her fault, nor mine that we are treated unfairly while others such as you are clearly favored."

Facing off against Tamyn's stare while she sat next to him, Deverin quickly lowered his gaze and turned quiet as he became visibly intimidated. However, his friend was not affected by it as she opened her mouth towards the older elf.

"It is quite comical that you think we have it easier," said Varissa. "You come from a privileged family and have had more schooling than any other here. It is not fair for you to be among us."

"Or that peasant girl who lowers our classroom's standards," added Deverin who joined in on Varissa's banter as he clearly felt stronger behind her voice.

"You may be right about me," said Tamyn as she turned to stare onto her two bantering peers. "But, only a coward projects outward insecurities towards a 'girl' who was able to summon a stone without a wand, a feat you were unable to do."

Despite the classroom's unhappiness towards their assignment, most began to cheer towards Cora and even shy away from Deverin and Varissa's argument.

Feeling she had the room's attention, Tamyn continued towards the mildly humiliated pair, "Perhaps you would make better use of this time by taking out your textbooks and studying, rather than wasting time on petty insults."

To Deverin and Varissa's dismay, the rest of the class supported Tamyn as they joined her in taking out some notes and books to prepare for the upcoming evaluation. Feeling as if they were silenced and disgraced, the two had no choice but to follow in a slight fit.

Turning around to face Cora, Tamyn provided her with a small set of notes that had scribbled spells on them. "Here, study this," she said. "These are incantations and words that will be covered in a few days."

Reluctant to take them, Cora deflected by asking, "But what'll you study?"

Referring to their two books that were still within the Instructor's desk, Tamyn said, "I do not require them, I can start reviewing next month's lesson ahead of time instead." Dropping the pieces of parchment onto Cora's desk, she continued, "As they said, I have had plenty of time before."

Setting aside her initial hesitation, Cora agreed and took them. Feeling somewhat shaken still by the vision, she first reached into her pack for Chirpy. After putting her comforting figurine out in front of her, she then began her silent review of Tamyn's materials.

As she started on the first few lines, Cora could not help but feel the words she read would trigger her wand's jewel and lead to another vision. Feeling safer if she put it away, she tucked it into the basket below her seat and carried on.

However, it did not appear to help much as Cora kept feeling rather distressed the more she read. She was concerned over the grey cloud and wanted to stay away from triggering another episode where she might see more of it alongside the dark figure. And so, she pushed the parchment away from her and instead, stared downward in thought into Chirpy's intricately carved, wooden frame.

Cora allowed nothing to distract her as she pondered deeply for a few moments while looking at her soothing toy, not even the footsteps she heard next to her that were followed by a rattling in the back, then the returning march.

In spite of her desires to be left alone while she calmed herself the best way she knew how, Cora's thoughts were interrupted when a large, bloated coat was thrust from her right.

"Here," said Deverin as he mockingly fluffed out the winged arms to increase its size. Throwing it over Cora, he then turned back to his desk and began scrunching several pieces of parchment into oval-shaped rings.

Although Cora remained silent and tried to resume her thoughts despite being shamed by the unrelenting pair, Tamyn grew visibly bothered. With a stern face, she asked Deverin, "Just what are you doing?"

"I am making ears and her cave," he responded. While turning around and presenting them to Cora, he continued, "For our Lesser Elf who set aside her wand and notes. This will help you look and feel like a Dwarf."

"Get that away from her," countered Tamyn as she ripped off the wide garment from her friend, then threw it onto Deverin's hands. "Leave her alone already and study."

Encouraged by Deverin that scornfully held the ears and coat, Varissa said, "Why? Soon she will turn the wand into a shovel and add the gem to her collection." Provoked by Cora's cheeks that grew rosy and her eyes that became watery, she further bantered, "She will become fat and ugly, forsaking all learning of magic as they did, so why stop us from letting the inevitable happen?"

Taking a firm stance, Tamyn stood to face the taller Deverin who was almost half a foot greater than her at six feet. Clearly not intimidated by the two elves that bullied her friend, she reiterated, "I said leave her alone."

"Or else what?" said Varissa who began laughing at Tamyn.

Nudged by his friend, Deverin leaned forward with the items he held and said, "This will help you dig away at the dirt like your parents."

Shoving the coat and ears towards Cora once more, Deverin did so while preoccupied with staring at Tamyn –

causing him to miss the human student's head and body. Instead, he landed the heavy coat onto her desk and crashed it into her toy, sending it flying off atop the hard tile.

As Chirpy's beak snapped on the floor and a part of its body chipped, Cora lunged forward and cried, "No!" Holding its broken parts together, she said while tears ran down her cheek, "Why? I said I'm sorry." Cradling her feet on the floor, she continued with a few sniffles, "I-I just want to go home."

For a brief moment, Tamyn only looked down at her weeping friend – stunned that the pair would continue to act so low towards her. Raising her head up, a rush of anger hit Tamyn as she grew flushed and balled her fists.

Although Deverin was silent at first over his actions, Varissa mockingly said, "Children's toys have no place here, anyhow."

Prompted by his friend, Deverin furthered, "It was your fault for being in the way. You…"

Infuriated at the pair that berated her friend, Tamyn reached for her wand and rose it up to Deverin's mouth rapidly to interrupt him as she said, "Draeyst."

With a small gust of wind, the very air from the male elf's lungs was purged outward – leaving him gasping and falling to the floor.

As her peer struggled to catch his breath, Varissa frantically said, "You attacked a student, in class! Everyone here saw it."

Raising her wand towards the shouting elf, Tamyn remarked towards Varissa, "Shall it be two, then? Or just him?"

"No, please," begged Varissa fervently in her cowardice. "I will study. Please, I promise."

Staring harshly towards the two bullies, Tamyn said, "Shut it already. Get back in your seat and leave us alone."

Struggling to lift himself up to his desk, Deverin took a moment before taking his seat while panting heavily. As both Varissa and he remained seated without another word, Tamyn drew her attention to Cora and went down to the floor next to her.

"Cora, come," she said. "Let us sit down on our chairs as well."

Still heartbroken from her shattered figurine, Cora said while sorrowfully looking downward, "Chirpy's broken. This was Poppa's gift to me when I turned five, now it's broken forever."

Seeing the value such a simple wooden carving held to her friend, Tamyn reassured, "We can fix Chirpy, I promise."

Wiping away a set of droplets from her rose-colored cheeks, Cora sniffled then said while looking up, "Can you?"

"Myself, I may not be able to," responded Tamyn, "but our family has friends who repair even the most complex of wands. I am certain they will happily do the same for a gift so dear to you."

After a nod of gratitude, Cora agreed to return to her seat. Slowly, she was lifted up by Tamyn amid a light cheer that caught them both by surprise.

Led by Mister Spearhawk at the front, more than half of the class let out a smile from their chairs that expressed a clear support for Tamyn and Cora.

Yet, it was apparent that Deverin and Varissa were against this sentiment as they visibly harbored a significant amount of frustration from their recent embarrassment. Quietly, they fixated themselves on their books and anxiously awaited their Instructor's return.

CHAPTER SIXTEEN:

"A PRACTICAL EXAM"

S trolling towards The School's entrance, Cora and her parents made their way together on this exciting, yet nerve-wracking day. It was a big moment for her, one where she was to be officially evaluated on the first few spells she had learned.

Yet, Cora's emotions were off. Feeling slightly down at times and mildly upbeat at others, her parents knew something was the matter in her schooling even though she had not spoken to them much about it.

Sensing this hesitation and odd silence, Aeyra tugged lightly at her daughter's hand while walking near the building's threshold and said, "Honey, if you're feeling a little nervous for the exam, don't be. You're as prepared as ever and it'll all be fine, you'll see."

"That's right, tulip," joined her father. "You'll be done in no time and we'll be celebrating with a special dinner just for you."

Although Cora was feeling down as she began to step in front of the elven guards, her spirits were slightly lifted as she then smiled and said, "Thank you, Momma. Poppa." Having just crossed the archway, she stopped in her tracks, then jumped onto her toes while her parents leaned down – allowing her to plant a kiss on both their cheeks while adding, "I love you."

As the three gave each other a warm embrace and began to bid their morning farewell, the two High Elf sentries did the unexpected and started looking at Cora. Caught by the odd encounter, she could not help but feel slightly uncomfortable, even timid.

Having noticed their daughter's fixation being returned by the two guards that were almost always motionless, the two parents stood upright and acknowledged them.

Being the concerned matriarch that she was, Aeyra was the first to ask, "Yes?"

After her short word, the two guards turned towards the mother, but only the left guard took a side step in front of the family.

With his firm stride finished, the moving guard then said in a rigid tone, "Everstones, with me if you will."

After feeling her daughter's rising tension, Aeyra was the first to question before her husband was even able to get out a mumbled sound. "Why?" she said. "Is there an issue?"

Bowing his head lightly, the left guard answered in his neutral voice, "Concern yourself not, my lady. The Head Instructor simply wishes to speak with your family in her office. She apologizes that she has been unable to sooner."

Before providing a response to the guard, the family turned to one another as they began to speak over themselves.

"We've got to be at the gardens soon," said Aeyra.

"You stay and see to her," offered Cehdric. "I'll get there early and get started until you're back."

"Are you certain?" asked Aeyra. "There's quite a bit to do."

"I'll handle it until then," responded Cehdric. With a cheerful smirk, he added, "At least, I think I can. No one's hands are quite as good as yours." Giving a wink to his child, he finished, "And it's just some silly garden, our tulip's affairs always come first."

Bending once more, Cehdric gave a gentle, caring embrace to his daughter, then lifted himself to share another with his wife before he began to walk off. As he then made his leave, the guard ushered in the mother and daughter with a silent acknowledgment.

Following the elven sentry closely, the pair went on a similar trail to Cora's new class. As they kept up the pace, the mother started offering encouraging words for her daughter's upcoming test as she noticed a few more nervous flutters along their way – ones she offered in a soft manner to be considerate for the somewhat quiet halls. She clearly desired to put her child at ease as best she could, but seemingly stopped short as the guard suddenly halted.

Having hit a forked passage, the elven attendant pointed to the left, while signaling Cora down her usual hallway towards her room.

With another gentle hug, Aeyra said before departing, "We're so proud of you, honey. We'll be right here to pick you up as soon as you're done today."

Although she wanted to extend her embrace, Cora knew she had to get going. After caressing her mother tightly, she let her go and shared a nod along with her goodbye. Leaving the guard with her parent, she then moved towards Ravenbeak's room and entered in silence.

She was quiet and so was the class, but many of them let off reassuring looks towards one they clearly now considered their peer. With a slight boost in her pride, she strode to her seat and settled herself in to briefly study while awaiting the rest of the students that trickled in.

As a few moments went by, Cora began to organize her desk – laying her wand out and clearing any notes she went over as she awaited class to begin. With Tamyn and one last student moving in, they shut the door to the class and assumed their desks.

Stepping down her aisle in front of Cora, Tamyn gave her friend a proud look and said while sitting down, "I wish you luck, although we shall be fine today."

Acknowledging her friend, Cora leaned in and whispered so as to not draw much attention. "Thank you for helping me," she said.

Desiring to speak further to her elven companion, Cora sat back and postured herself as she saw the Instructor lifting himself up and stepping in front of his desk as he did when he was about to initiate his announcements.

"Class," Ravenbeak announced in a resentful tone. "It appears there are those of you who are not satisfied with this course and its instruction. Your complaints have been heard, yet those grievances will do nothing to alter my schedule and methods for this curriculum. This assessment has, and always will, remain fair and impartial to the abilities of the student. So if there are those of you who feel you are being treated unfairly, I ask you to speak up now."

Hearing this, Cora deep down wanted to speak up, but could not muster the strength to do so since she noticed her stoic friend, Tamyn, also remain quiet despite her recent, more talkative mood. With Tamyn's silence, she felt there was a reason for it, so she too, followed.

With all of the students not uttering a word, Ravenbeak continued, "Just as I assumed. Since none of you care to add to our morning's dialogue, we shall then move forward with the practical assessment."

Taking a few steps over to a closet that sat by his desk, the Instructor pulled its latches open and revealed a wooden target that he rolled out. After propping it up in the center of the class, he announced, "Mister Spearhawk, forward please."

Climbing out of his desk, the young elf student took a pace off to the side, then awaited his instruction.

"Mister Spearhawk," resumed Ravenbeak while pointing to the stick held in the target's hands, "you shall disarm this wand. When you are ready, you may proceed."

Preparing himself, the calm pupil brought his own weapon to the center of his chest, then extended it outward as he recited, "Detawlamh."

Successfully, he forced the wand out of the mark's clutches, then moved forward to reset the wooden piece as the Instructor said, "Good, next."

Calling the students down aisle by aisle and row by row in his typical fashion, Ravenbeak went through the line where Cora would, as always, be last. As each peer went before her, she began to feel more flutters in her stomach and jitters along her arms. She saw as different incantations were called upon – from basic strikes, to glows and beams, followed by even more disarming spells. It was all seemingly random to her and it removed any hope of anticipating what she would be asked to perform.

In spite of the irregular pattern of spells, Cora still knew all the words of each enchantment that was said before her. She was prepared and ready as her parents, even Tamyn had said. But, she still felt hesitant and even slightly fearful of using her wand – so she kept it as far as she could from her reach on her desk until she would be called upon.

Having now gone onto her aisle and just a few seats in front, Cora knew she would be asked to rise soon. Her tension built and her anxiety worsened as a light sweat grew on her while she watched the student before Tamyn go.

Now moving to the penultimate trainee, Ravenbeak called in a somewhat sarcastic manner, "Miss Starborne, if you would grace us with your presence."

Unbothered with the Instructor's tone, Tamyn calmly lifted herself up and readied her wand.

Reacting unkindly and dismissive as he had done before, Ravenbeak began to circle around his serene student, then said, "A short, pulse of air if you would – move the target back." While Cora and the rest of the class reacted surprisingly to the unanticipated request, he continued, "That is, if you know such a specific spell from your 'advanced' studies. If not, you may proceed with a standard disarming spell for a lower grade."

Collected and proud as ever, Tamyn nodded and simply said, "As you wish." Taking her aim, she moved her slender wand down her sights then called aloud, "Aurawerian."

As the wheels of the wooden target rattled while it was sent back, Tamyn's fellow students, particularly Cora, cheered loudly as she used an air spell that was not part of their recent studies.

When the rear boards of the base slammed into the classroom's door, Tamyn said, "I hope it was to your satisfaction."

"Hmph," reacted the Instructor as he then dismissed Tamyn to her seat.

Walking back confidently to her desk, Tamyn gave an encouraging nod to Cora as she was then called as the last student.

"Miss Everstone," said the Instructor to break the two friends' stare. "If you would care to join us."

Grasping her wand that looked bigger in her hands than anyone else's, Cora shifted out of her chair, then began walking forward.

She was as nervous as ever, but she was eased by Tamyn's whisper. "You can do it," she said in a low voice with her hand over her mouth so as not to unnecessarily alert the teacher.

With her anxiety lessened, Cora slightly tilted her head upward from having paced with her head down as she moved past the third, then second, and lastly, the first chair of the aisle. Making short steps to the front of the class, she then looked up at the Instructor who had his eyes beading down onto her.

Though she was calmer than before, she was at the front and center of the room – an imposing, even overwhelming sight that created a heavier feeling in her gut. Yet, she readied herself the same, bringing her wand forward in a mildly jittery motion and at the ready as she awaited her exhibition.

"Miss Everstone," proceeded the Instructor in a malcontent voice, "I understand you are quite familiar with certain woods and how they break and crack." Pointing at a fissure in the target, he said, "Repair the gap and mend its wounds."

Visibly, Cora was bothered by the request as she put her head down and could only recall Chirpy being recently broken. The memory of her comforting toy being thrown onto the tile caused her to look downward with a somber expression. As a slew of bad memories, from being bullied to the nightmarish visions poured in, she started to hesitate further and grow a despaired look.

"Miss Everstone," said the perturbed Instructor who clearly did not care for his student's emotions, "we do not have all day. Your spell or take a seat."

Lifting her head, she was anxious but then she started to remember all the recent good as she glanced over at the smiling Tamyn. In an instant, she recalled that those who pestered their friendship were beat back and how promises for a bright future were looming upon them both as their families had been getting along so well lately.

Feeling renewed, Cora shuffled her feet, then lifted her wand. She closed her eyes at first, but opened them to stare at the broken segment. Looking down at it intensely, she took a breath and said, "Deigronan."

Sending a ripple into the wood, the crack began to gleam as parts of it began to sloppily sow itself back together. It was not as well as she would have hoped, but the fissure started to join itself nonetheless.

However, as the magic started to do its work, Cora saw a small hint of grey dust pour out of the wound. With another spout, a line of darkened air began to seep outward alongside a larger cloud that followed it and soon engulfed her surroundings.

As she let out a surprised yelp and raised her hands upward to shield her face, Cora saw a bright red glow that burst outward – ripping apart the whirlwind and sending it away from her.

Rubbing her lids, she tried to remove any of the dust she thought may have gotten into her eyes, but she felt nothing – not a single ounce anywhere.

Startled by its effect, she then looked up, but saw to her dismay, the sun peeking through a set of gloomy clouds.

Shocked once more at its sight, she looked around her and saw only grass atop a hill and the kneeling figure of the one she had come to know as the High General, who was nestled atop the ground.

With a grunt, the High General lifted himself up to Cora's side, although he appeared to not notice her presence as usual. An arrow was stuck in his leg along with a bright crimson and grey stain on his golden armor where the Head Instructor's gem once was. He was covered with sweat and dirt; visibly exhausted, beaten, and alone. Yet, he still stood valiant, ready to fight as he pointed his sword and shield forward.

Following the action, Cora brought her wand at the ready and aimed it towards the approaching figure that continued towards their position.

They watched in a silent, but alarmed state as the ashy cloak of the mysterious person bounced up and down atop his darkened, padded armor that was wrapped in layers of cloth and linen. He appeared as a shrouded traveler, one armed with a serrated sword and a hooked sickle at his side.

Although she was clearly more scared than the High General, Cora still stood strong – holding her wand with two hands outward and trying her best to lessen the shaking that emanated down her wrists.

She was anxious, wondering who or what this ominous figure was, just as the High General did.

Yet, their questions were soon answered as the figure slightly removed his shroud – revealing a set of long, pale ears as a Dark Elf would have.

Pausing his steps, the sinister elf looked towards the High General and said in an arrogant tone, "So this is the one who drives the banner of those who dare stand against me." Proudly, he boasted, "You are out of tricks. Surrender and you may live."

164

After a cough, the High General responded, "My life is no more important than all those you and your rabble have threatened in your pursuit of fracturing the peace." While quickly snapping the part of the arrow shaft that protruded from his leg, he then resumed his defensive posture and taunted, "If you want me to submit, come and claim my blade. Then, I may consider it."

Irritated by his words, the Dark Elf lunged forward with his weapons and clashed against the raised shield of the High General. As they dueled, Cora raised her wand forward and tried to cast a magical strike, but nothing happened. Helplessly, she could only stand by as the two fought while she remained tethered to the High General's side.

Although he was visibly more strained, the High General stopped every blow and even countered with a few bashes from his shield – sending the evil elf backwards.

"You dare contest me?" spouted the Dark Elf who was more focused on words than his own combat. "You are outmatched, beaten."

While clashing his blade, the High General used the distraction and maneuvered himself to strike his opponent near his neck with the bottom of his hilt – sending him fumbling backwards.

Bruising his adversary, the High General chuckled and said, "Then why have you not taken my blade yet?"

Infuriated by the comment, the evil elf rushed forward and attacked in a frenzy. He clashed and swung both of his weapons while shouting aloud, "How dare you defy me? Do you not know who I am? Whose wrath you have incurred?"

"No," answered the High General as he returned and deflected each blow, "nor do I care. You threaten our peace and the balance, you are just another enemy to the free people that shall be brought to justice."

"Agh!" shouted the Dark Elf in frustration as he pulled back to unleash a wave of dark magic that forced the High General to fall down. As his shield fell to the side, the malicious elf used another silent incantation to decompose the superior wood and metal board to ash.

With only his sword left, the High General raised himself up and continued to fight bravely until the Dark Elf used another form of wordless dark magic to heat the blade and hilt – forcing it to drop from his hands.

Having no weapon available to him, the High General was forced to his knees as his attacker roughly pushed him down onto the ground. Disarmed and helpless, he only watched as the evil elf gloated.

"Submit," said the Dark Elf. "Surrender yourself and the artifact, then you shall receive my mercy."

Although he was prompted to respond, the High General only laughed.

Obviously insulted and angered, the malicious elf yelled out, "You mock me?"

"No," answered the High General. As several horns of his people and allies rang from all around their position, he continued, "I merely distract you."

Shackling the High General with a spell that tightly bound him, the Dark Elf pressed to the golden box amid the resounding horns that only agitated him further. As he then smashed the lock, he opened the container to reveal a well-lined chest that was entirely empty.

Restrained and disarmed, the High General was only able to use words as his armament. Speaking to the thwarted villain in a content manner, he said, "You may have claimed me, yet four armies now descend upon you – to crush your northern legions. Surrender, and I shall grant you the same mercy that you offered me."

In a fit of rage, the Dark Elf incinerated the golden chest with a foul magic, then turned to the High General. Setting his eyes upon the one who fooled him, he spouted angrily, "I am merciless, unseen, and you have done nothing but incur my everlasting wrath this day!" Thrusting his weapons upward and charging forward, he continued, "I will curse you for all eternity. Not just you, but your entire bloodline and all those who have ever supported you!"

With the blades bearing down upon them, the High General only stared upward with a gleaming hope in his eyes but Cora screamed aloud in panic. Although she stood by him, she did not share the same courage he let off as she was not accustomed to such a chaotic threat. Her fright and despair soon propounded, growing worse when the Dark Elf let off a last set of words as he initiated a slash while looking back and forth towards the two.

"The Starbornes will end, fading into nothingness by my divine will!" shouted the sinister elf while letting off a malevolent gaze.

Unable to look, Cora closed her eyes when the blow came crashing down, but she heard, felt, and sensed nothing as she could only fall backwards in fear. As she landed, she touched a hardened, stony ground that was cold and polished. She heard her wand tumble and roll between her feet in a smooth motion – one not indicative of the grass she thought she was on. Then it came, a slew of safe and familiar sounds, of concerned students who started to ask about what had just occurred before their very eyes.

"The end of the Starbornes?"

"Why would she say that?"

"Is she well?"

"She saw something, look at her," they said as they pointed to their distraught peer.

Shocked and visibly frightened by her experience, Cora only cried and shivered amid the awed stares – ignoring all else as she remained seated in a state of distress atop the classroom's tile.

CHAPTER SEVENTEEN:

"VISIONS GONE BY"

"Cora, stay with me," comforted Tamyn emotionally as she held her distraught friend. "You are safe," she reassured.

After the ominous display following her peer's spell, Tamyn – without hesitation and regard for the Instructor – rushed to the front of the classroom and cradled Cora through the disarray. With a great concern and more emotion than she had ever displayed, she attempted every act she knew in order to calm the panicked child that cried relentlessly.

"He killed him," Cora said in a wailing voice as she was held, "the High General, he's dead and I couldn't do anything. I tried."

As all listened in with their own opinions, Tamyn tuned them out and focused on Cora as she said to her, "There is nothing you could have done. You saw a moment in the past, yet I am here with you now."

"But the bad elf saw me," said the teary-eyed Cora. "He's coming for you and me – he said your name."

"Nothing is coming for us here," remarked Tamyn while trying to further soothe her friend. As a watery film grew on her own eyes from the memory of her fallen relative, she continued, "The evil that took my kin from us was defeated almost immediately after on that same field. My grandfather had sacrificed himself so our people could live, we are safe."

"But what if he escaped?" said the whimpering Cora. "He was a Dark Elf, the big scary bird, the dark cloud. He didn't even need to say a word to use spells, so what if he's disguised like someone else now? Looking for us."

Pondering on Cora's words, Tamyn reflected inward for a moment on what to say next, but her delay prompted the Instructor to join them.

"Fascinating," he said in his interruption. In an uncaring manner, he furthered while staring down onto Cora, "It would appear the Grand Magister was correct all along, she has seen someone special indeed – perhaps the sixth."

Primarily focused on the first part Ravenbeak spewed from his mouth, Tamyn became angered. Looking over to her insensitive teacher that lacked any compassion, she said, "Have you no sympathy? She is haunted by visions of your High General and all you are is 'fascinated' with it?"

Condescendingly, the Instructor responded, "Intrigued, interested... it all means the same when referring to a former battle commander's demise."

Having emphasized his words when describing her grandfather, Tamyn grew infuriated. In a passionate fit, she shouted towards him, "You are an ungrateful, selfish fool just like your blind leader." Trying hard to force herself to calm slightly, she then gazed at Cora and said, "Come, we need to get you to the Head Instructor immediately." As her friend struggled to move, she encouraged, "You need rest, to be taken to your mother and father at home." Gently, she finished while handing Cora back her nearby wand, "We will go slowly, but I need your help to get us there."

Following Cora's soft, shy nod, Tamyn helped her up. As they stood by each other, Tamyn began to turn towards the door but was halted by the Instructor's rude reaction.

"How dare you presume what she needs," rambled the Instructor as he went towards the room's only exit. "You are not going anywhere with the Grand Magister's student."

"The Head Instructor's student, you mean," remarked Tamyn firmly. "The one who cares for us all in The School, unlike you."

Acting rather offended by the comment, Ravenbeak harshly said, "I will hear no more of this! Astrael is second to him, only Davik's authority matters inside and outside of these walls."

In a determined motion, the Instructor pushed the closed door tight and went over to his desk where his wand sat. As he crossed Tamyn, he brushed by her shoulder in a pompous manner while he looked down onto her with an irritated expression. After reaching over his chair, he said, "You will learn, one way or the other."

As the Instructor spun around with his wand that was held low, he saw Tamyn already pointing her own weapon at him while the other arm held Cora upright.

"No," Tamyn said as she bore her wand onto Ravenbeak, "you will." Flicking her wrist, she chanted aloud, "Revabaed."

With a rapid force of air that burst outward, the Instructor was sent tumbling backwards and over his desk – landing just behind it while his wand slipped away from his grasp.

Urging Cora to move, Tamyn shifted her friend towards the door and said, "Come on!"

Her first pace was slow, but Cora eventually picked up and followed Tamyn fast enough with her help. Stepping past the threshold of the room, the two rushed into the halls amid the screams of the Instructor who yelled for any to stop them.

At first, Tamyn did not hear anyone behind them as she was so focused on keeping her friend upright, but then she felt a magical bolt zip by her that slammed onto the nearby walls. As the weak, poorly aimed strike landed, she lowered her head then turned around while placing herself in front of Cora.

Extending her wand out, she shouted, "Stay behind me!" As another missile was fired towards them, she calmly said, "Hildaest."

Seemingly more powerful than her attacker, Tamyn was easily able to shatter the incoming bolt with her shield that split it into bits. As her blocking spell withdrew with a white light, she aimed outward and saw Varissa approaching with Deverin just behind.

"You attacked an Instructor!" said Deverin from slightly afar.

"Stop your running," followed Varissa as she held her wand out steady in her march.

Seeing Varissa wind up once more in a fancy motion, the speedier Tamyn countered with a simple aim before a third attack could be fired upon them. "Naciuin," she said while angling her arm at her younger peer.

Being more experienced, Tamyn easily disabled Varissa's voice, then set herself onto the baffled Deverin, spouting aloud, "Detawlamh."

As his wand was sent flying from his hand, Deverin went frantically crying down the hallway – chasing after his weapon in a panicked state and away from his fellow classmate that was clearly more skilled than he.

For a brief moment, Tamyn was relieved as no other students followed outward, but before she could continue onward to the Head Instructor's office, a greater threat emerged – forcing her to posture herself.

Enraged from the display, the Instructor did not hesitate to send a powerful strike soaring towards Tamyn's quickly erected shield.

As the blow was barely deflected, Ravenbeak boasted, "You are outmatched, yield." Before even allowing his pupil time to get a word out, he sent another attack forth – this time penetrating the shield and forcing Tamyn to backpedal with Cora.

Mildly, Tamyn screamed in pain as the Instructor wound himself back for another spell. Her shielding enchantment had already failed her, yet she did not give off the slightest notion of surrendering. Decisively, she looked to her friend, then back to her adversary as she renewed her protective incantation.

This time, to her surprise, she was accompanied by the meekly uttered words of Cora. With her wand barely held out, the brave child joined her friend in a low voice as she said, "Hildaest."

Having doubled their barrier, the shocking lance that was hurled violently towards Tamyn and Cora was repelled, but just barely as most of it still pierced through.

Growing weaker from their extended use of magic and losing their footing, Tamyn knew they could not withstand another volley. Once more, she looked to Cora, who was now as fragile as ever. Watching as her friend's eyes closed and her body trembled, she said, "I am sorry."

Gloating, the Instructor went forward as he said arrogantly, "You are beaten."

After a quick moment of boasting, the Instructor then aimed another outward spell to subdue those who stood against him, but he unexpectedly stopped, then created his own blocking incantation.

Shocked by the defensive maneuver, Tamyn looked to her Instructor in confusion as she did not cast a spell while she sheltered her friend from harm. Before she could even ponder over the matter, she heard a faint voice from behind – one that unleashed a flurry of fiery attacks towards Ravenbeak.

After a heavy burst of flame and smoke, Tamyn stared on as the Instructor's shield was diminished, then consumed entirely by the unrelenting assault – one that eventually forced him to shriek as a burning pain set in on his hands.

Having finished his mild outcry, the Instructor shouted out in Tamyn and Cora's direction, although he did so while staring over them. Clearly focused on the one who aided the two, he said, "Step aside for your superior's sake, leave them." While holding his aching wrist, he continued even louder in a visible frustration as the steps behind Tamyn and Cora only grew closer, "She will belong to him now after what has transpired, you cannot stop it! You have failed her!"

As Ravenbeak's last word was uttered, a familiar red robe swayed just past Tamyn's arm. Confidently pacing herself towards her subordinate, the Arch Magister made her entrance known as she responded.

"No," the Head Instructor said, "it is you who have failed your students." As other teachers and pupils began to peek their head outwards from their classrooms, she continued, "Our students do not belong to anyone but to themselves." Breaking her speech for a moment, she used a disarming spell to send Ravenbeak's wand away from him, then she went on,

"We are here for them, to teach them, to watch them grow and become what they were meant to be – not to treat them as property."

"You and your morals," said the Instructor in his resentful outburst. "They will be the death of you, or at least should have been on that very day your precious High General died."

Rather than react passionately, Astrael instead calmly said, "You are finished. For your continued defiance and having assaulted students within The School, you shall waste away – jailed within the Golden Cells."

Although Ravenbeak attempted to shout out against his superior, he was quieted and put to sleep through a Somaedh spell that forced him to fall back on his feet. As he fainted onto the floor, two more pairs of steps emerged from behind Tamyn. The first, of plated boots as a Highguard would wear, marched steadily towards the Instructor with orders to arrest him, while the second one of lighter soles stuttered their steps, and then rapidly rushed to the two huddled students.

With overwhelming emotion, the second figure embraced Tamyn and Cora from behind, then revealed her familiar voice.

"Cora, honey," said the overly concerned Aeyra as she startled her daughter awake. "Are you alright? Please tell me you're alright."

Not hesitating, Cora immediately held her mother's arms that wrapped around her as she cried, "Momma!" With a slew of droplets rolling down her eyes, she started to vividly recall certain moments of fright she just saw. Yet, she was stopped before much was said of the dark figure coming for her – halted by Astrael as she joined the three.

Focusing onto Cora, the Head Instructor said, "Miss Everstone, I apologize as we again have not much time. You must come with me." Looking to Tamyn and Aeyra, she urged, "All of you." Directing herself only to Tamyn, she finished, "You know where we must go."

Insisting they move, the Head Instructor turned everyone down the hall and towards the exit. She was brief in her words, but what she did say managed to stress the urgency of their situation and how they needed to vacate The School's grounds before the Grand Magister's impending arrival due to the recent events.

In support of the pressing swiftness instilled by the Head Instructor, Tamyn began to reassure Cora and her mother of their destination – adding that it would be a safe location for them as it was her own home and part of a recently devised contingency should it be required.

"We can help you there," said Tamyn as they approached the outside. "And you can rest."

Knowing only a portion of the details spoken between her own parents and the Arch Magister, Tamyn was mildly astonished when she saw a large formation of Highguards that faced away from them with a small pocket in their middle.

Ushering them inward and under the cover of the tall pikes, the Head Instructor said, "Stay inside and keep up with the march."

Lifting her daughter up with all of her might, Aeyra carried Cora in first, followed by Tamyn and Astrael who joined in before the guarded formation locked itself.

As the surrounding elves began to pace forward, the Head Instructor said to the other three huddled within, "The gathering crowd we assembled along with the marching files will keep us hidden for some time."

While trying her best to keep up with the steps as she held her child, the troubled mother asked, "For what? I need to know."

"Please," said the Head Instructor as she noticed Aeyra's steps slow while her panicked state built up, "it is as we just discussed moments ago. I promise, we will elaborate further when we are safe and your husband has joined us. For now, we need to keep up until we reach the gate."

Although even Tamyn was curious to ask what the rest of the plan was, she kept silent as the rest now did – focusing solely on their steps. They did so in good time as soon, it started to become more difficult with the number of those around them steadily growing. As their own concentration started to wain in light of the multitude of surrounding people, the Highguards by their side chanted a helpful cadence to aid them in their rhythmic movement.

Unsure of how much longer they could hold this, Tamyn started to feel the anxiety that surrounded Aeyra, but was relieved when one of the forward soldiers signaled their arrival. Turning their file, they opened the rear ranks of their formation in a coordinated fashion and allowed the four to drop out into the crossing that led to the southwestern housing section.

Pushing just past its gated threshold, the Head Instructor said as she led on, "Quickly, this way." Begging they follow her, she took them to a nearby, small carriage that was driven by two horses. Guiding the others into the decorated and covered coach, she then signaled the awaiting driver to press rapidly towards the home of the Starbornes.

In little time, the four arrived at their destination that already held the door slightly open for them. As discreet as she could, the Head Instructor then escorted everyone inside and shut the door with the aid of the Starborne matriarch who stood by.

Being the first to greet them, Amalyn said, "I apologize we are meeting under these circumstances." Setting her eyes onto the distraught Cora, she added, "Let us find you somewhere to rest where we can bring you some comfort."

Pointing down the hall, Amalyn directed Aeyra to a cozy seating arrangement, one where Cora could lie down atop a few pillowed decorations.

Without hesitating as she was only concerned for her child, Aeyra did as she was requested. As she set her daughter down, a few tears rolled down her eyes as Cora began to repeat the same phrase.

"Momma," said the tormented Cora. "He's coming, I saw him again when I closed my eyes. He's coming."

"Who, tulip," cried Aeyra. "Who!?"

"He's bad," responded Cora as her mother wiped away a few drops from her reddened face that ceaselessly wept. "He's coming for us."

While Cora continued on in her frightened state, Tamyn was pulled aside by her mother and the Arch Magister.

"Tamyn," asked Amalyn, "what did she tell you of what she saw?"

As she recited the description Cora gave of the pale traveler who shifted shapes and used a constant stream of wordless magic, both her mother and the Head Instructor gasped.

"Then it is true," said the worried Arch Magister in a low voice so that Aeyra and Cora could not hear. "He is the one who claimed Baydyn." As Amalyn and Tamyn let out a bleak, unspoken acknowledgment, she continued, "Davik and Limrich's recent interest in these matters now make sense, although it does not excuse their actions." Pausing for a second to gulp, she finished, "Yet it matters not. We have precautions in place as we have always had."

Joining the three, Aeyra said in a distraught manner while alluding to her panicked daughter, "What's going to happen to her?" Pointing at Cora who repeated several of the same lines while crying to herself, she whispered emotionally, "It's worse than ever, she's…"

Interrupted by the resounding door that opened and closed, Aeyra only stopped momentarily as Cehdric rushed in with an increasingly worried look. After grabbing a hold of her husband, she went on in a demanding manner that expressed clear concern for her child, "She needs help now. None of this schooling for years, or watching her, we need to do something this very moment." Gazing over to her child, she continued, "This one's the most disastrous yet and we can't let her suffer like this. Please, you need to help her now."

While lowering her own tone to impart calmness to the rest, the Head Instructor said, "You are right, she indeed needs our immediate attention. But I will need your permission first."

"Anything," blurted out Aeyra as Cehdric nodded alongside her.

"This is not a simple request," continued the Head Instructor. "Miss Everstone, Cora, has seen a traumatic event that still links itself to her somehow. To sever her from it will require a powerful spell, one that will not only part her from what she has seen, but likely more. Perhaps months, even years of memories. Are you prepared for that?"

Turning to her child, then back towards the Head Instructor, Aeyra tearfully said, "You've already told us we can't bear the pain on her behalf and schooling just isn't helping as fast as we'd have wanted, so what other choice do we have? Cehdric and I can't just stand by and watch her continue on in agony."

"She's our little tulip," said Cehdric as he let a few teardrops run down his cheek. "Even if she forgets who we are, we'll always be there for her – to remind her how much we love her, throughout every waking moment if we have to."

Although she was a stalwart High Elf, even Astrael was touched by the compassionate parents as she sniffled in her response. "She will never forget that," she said. "Your love will always be with her. However, she will likely forget her schooling, her move from Riverbend, and all recent events." Gazing onto Tamyn, she furthered, "Including her friendships." Continuing to the group, she went on, "And there shall be consequences from the Grand Magister that even I cannot avoid." Going on in a softer voice, she said, "In his disturbed mind, he prizes this vision and her abilities to see them as he has done with all Farseers. If I am to do this, I will be forced to resign my position and unable to see to Cora, even Tamyn's future within The School." Sensing the doubt from the Everstone parents, she clarified, "Yes, Cora will have to continue her studies, though she will have more time to master her abilities and possibly even control what she sees. Her link to magic, as much as one would desire, can never be truly severed."

While she expressed her concern for Cora, Amalyn also had doubts as she asked, "Are you certain this is the way?"

Taking in a breath, Astrael thoughtfully responded, "This is our only option where we can give Cora the time she needs, less we give her up to Davik who will only exploit her trauma here and now. We cannot hide her forever from him." Placing her hand on the Starborne matriarch, she continued in a consoling manner, "Baydyn once sacrificed himself for me and for a countless number of people. If my burden is to be exiled from teaching so that a kind, caring child can thrive, then so be it. I shall retire to Brightfork near his memorial and watch from afar."

Letting off a thankful expression, Amalyn said towards Astrael, "Although we remain here in this city, you shall not be alone."

"And neither will Cora," added Tamyn as she insisted the focus remain on her friend. As the Everstone parents' eyes gleamed of a growing joy, she furthered, "I will be there for her just like you shall. In class, as her peer, as her friend. Always."

Knowing their course of action, all turned to Cora as they knelt and stood near her in a calm, peaceful manner. As the closest ones to her, Aeyra held her daughter's hand and encircled her arms around her while Cehdric caressed the top of her head and hair.

"Honey," said Aeyra, "we're going to make you feel better."

Opening her eyes, Cora blinked away a few tears, then turned to her mother as she said sobbingly, "You're making him go away?"

"Yes, honey," answered Aeyra in a somber, yet hopeful tone.

In a similar manner to his wife, Cehdric added, "He'll leave our little tulip alone and go away for good."

After letting out a light groan as she turned to her parents, Cora softly said, "Thank you, Momma... Poppa." Changing her tone slightly, she asked in a mildly pleading manner, "Could you stay with me a little today? If it won't get you in trouble at work."

"Of course," responded Aeyra amid a few sobs. "We're not leaving you." Looking up at the others, she continued, "No one is, we'll all be here."

Despite her somber mood, Cora let out a cheerful smile that caused all the rest around her to share with their own happy grin. As she gently tilted her head to gaze up at Tamyn,

Cora followed, "I'm sorry, I tried but I couldn't. I wasn't strong enough."

"Oh, but you were," said Tamyn in a tranquil tone lined with encouragement. "We escaped with your aid and you even saved me from the Instructor, I should be thanking you."

"I did?" asked Cora in a bewildered manner.

"Yes," affirmed Tamyn. "I would be in the infirmary if not for you. Instead, I am here alongside you where we can study and share a bite to eat after you rest up and relax."

"Momma," said Cora as she turned to face her mother. "After I sleep a little, can we stay a bit longer?"

Once again, Aeyra answered, "Yes, honey."

"And we'll also get you some treats later from Mister Honeydew," said Cehdric as he joined in.

"But for now," added Aeyra, "try to close your eyes and get some rest. You've had quite a long morning." Sitting down onto the floor next to her daughter, she went on while holding her, "I'll be right here, keeping you safe with Poppa."

Turning over slightly, Cora softly said, "Thank you, Momma. Poppa. I love you."

Being near exhaustion from the troubling vision and the use of magical spells earlier, Cora's eyes easily shut after her parents gave her a warmhearted kiss. As her thoughts were now soothed, her mind began to drift from all of her worries as she only focused on the inviting and comforting darkness that surrounded her lids. While closing them tight and feeling the sensation of sleep coming on, she saw a flash of light that followed the faint voices of the Head Instructor and Tamyn's mother as they simultaneously said, "Doblideur."

-THE END-

The REALMS OF ERDARIS Series will continue with…

SERIES TITLES

Volume One
A FLOWER AMONG THE GOLD

Volume Two
FORGOTTEN IN THE ASHES

Volume Three
FATE OF WATER AND WIND

Volume Four
THE JADE DRAGONHEART

Volume Five
THE GRAND FORGES

Volume Six
THE LIFE CHRONICLES

Volume Seven
THE SHADOW'S MARK

Titles will be available online and at your local bookstore

Please visit the REALMS OF ERDARIS Series by Michael Patrick on Amazon & Goodreads for upcoming release information, author bio, and more. Join us on social media through Facebook, Instagram, & Twitter for the latest details.